TRANSITS

Betty Lundsted

TRANSITS

The Time of Your Life

SAMUEL WEISER, INC.

York Beach, Maine

First published in 1980 by
Samuel Weiser, Inc.
Box 612
York Beach, ME 03910

Seventh printing, 1992

Library of Congress Catalog Card Number: 83-159289

ISBN 0-87728-503-9
MG

Cover art © Michael Martin, 1989

Printed in the United States of America

The paper used in this publication meets the minimum requirements of the
American National Standard for Permanence of Paper for Printed Library
Materials Z39.48-1984.

Contents

This book is dedicated to the students who are looking for answers to the questions.

My thanks go to Ms. Chart A and Mr. Chart B for allowing me to use their charts.

The Time of Your Life

a time to be born and a time to die;
a time to plant and a time to uproot;
a time to kill and a time to heal;
a time to pull down and a time to build up;
a time to weep and a time to laugh;
a time for mourning and a time for dancing;
a time to scatter stones and a time to gather them;
a time to embrace and a time to refrain from embracing;
a time to seek and a time to lose;
a time to keep and a time to throw away;
a time to tear and a time to mend;
a time for silence and a time for speech;
a time to love and a time to hate;
a time for war and a time for peace.

(Ecclesiastes, 3)

People are very similar and yet very different. We are born, we live through the phases that encompass growing up. We are child, youth, adult; we fall in love, we have children or not, we grow old. We each respond to life differently. The symbolism contained in the natal chart shows us the potential for the differences between us. The transits of the planets show us our *timing*. We can observe the normal crisis periods, as well as our own personal crises, by watching our transits. We can better work with these crisis periods by understanding what causes them. Transits tell us how long the pressure will last and they allow us to comprehend what we are learning about ourselves so we can begin to use the energy constructively.

The creativity inherent in the human species can remain virtually untapped because we don't know that it exists. Some people are preoccupied with survival; some are preoccupied with "putting out fires" so that their time is spent cleaning up the messes they've created. If we can look at an upcoming transit period equipped with some understanding of what is about to happen, we can eventually get in touch with the creativity within, for we will be more free to use it. Using transits constructively can be likened to taking a walk in the rain wearing a raincoat and having an umbrella. People dressed for the rain are not bothered by it nearly as much as those who have been caught unprepared!

Transits basically signify important periods in the life. They activate the natal chart. A transit brings energy to some part of the personality and causes a change in consciouness to take place within an individual. A transit can set off natal complexes or aspects bringing attention to certain aspects of personality. The focus of attention can be either easy or difficult but that depends on the natal chart as well as how you've worked with it up until this point. For example, a Jupiter transit may signify a period of opportunity, but that opportunity may not be easily recognized if the transit also activates a natal Mars-square-Sun. Instead, it will energize the natal aspect, and until the natal condition is understood, the person with the Jupiter transit may not be able to see the opportunities available.

Transits signify periods of growth. If we wish to use the transit period for our growing, we need to begin when the seeds of the transit are planted. First the ground has to be tilled, then the seeds are planted—and even if we don't want potatoes, we may have to oversee the crop. Many students attempt to interpret a transit when it is basically over, for they begin to work with it when the crop is being harvested. The unpleasant crop harvested from a difficult transit occurs when we haven't been aware of the effect of a transit soon enough.

For that reason, when charting upcoming transits, I use a ten degree applying orb. In that way, the energy can be transformed with knowledge and understanding. The sextiles and trines are not of major importance because we don't usually need help handling them. We need some help with the hard aspects—for they force growth. The growth period allows you to weed your crop; you can make sure it doesn't catch worms or blight. The timing factor in the life becomes something that each of us has some control over and this eliminates the feeling of being victimized. The timing of the life experience then becomes exciting rather than something to fear or dread.

This book is an outgrowth of classes. My students liked learning how to use transits in a constructive sense. They liked the idea of taking hold of the life experience. Working with transits is like learning how to drive a car—once you learn how, it's fun. Several prerequisites are required, however. You must take responsibility for yourself. And you must give up the idea of prediction. Many astrologers love to predict the future. But if we take responsibility for our actions, the future becomes difficult to predict with accuracy. Gloom and doom will only happen if we insist on making it happen. Rough transits usually mean an ill-tended garden—or perhaps a crop you didn't know how to raise. That can be remedied with understanding.

Students learn about the concept of progressions and transits by working backward in the life of some famous person. If we take Richard Nixon's life, for example, and we work with his chart, we can see the timing for certain political moves that he made. And we can say that under such and such transit or progressed aspect, the man was promoted, or elected, or whatever. However, when attempting to do a reading for an average client, how can you do that?

How can you predict the future for a construction worker or a secretary? How do you read for an ordinary person? And if you didn't know you were talking to Richard Nixon, what would you say to him? If he came to you and said he was Joe Blow, could you see the presidential nomination in his chart? I don't think so.

You don't know your client's education, his background, his work history. You don't know the decisions he made under previous cycles or transits. Those decisions can alter the effect of a contemporary transit. You don't know whether he is using his energy constructively or not. So when reading for a total stranger, the astrolger is placed in a predicament. Some astrologers have what is known as psychic ability, and they use it to call the shots. Some just resort to guessing, and sometimes their guesses really frighten a client or some of the guesses just make people laugh at astrology because the reader is so wrong.

This system of transits works whether you know a client or not. You can talk to a total stranger about his life and the decisions he will be making in the coming year. You don't have to know what his occupation is, although you might be better able to talk to him if you know something about his education or career goals. He can interpret what you say so that he can apply the information to any life crisis in his future.

When I first started to study astrology, I found the idea of progressions rather confining. Transits were primarily ignored for they were only used in a one-to-three degree orb. This meant that a Saturn transit would be applying for a week or two, perhaps a month. I was learning that events were rather predestined, although I also heard that the "stars don't compel." Being a student of metaphysics, I was somewhat perplexed, for metaphysical theories delve into the possibility of changing the future. I learned that under a Saturn transit, for example, we could expect very little. The ideas confused me.

Along with the pessimistic view of hard aspects, I was learning the transits backwards. I resisted that idea because I wanted to learn how to read forward. People don't come for readings to hear about what they've already done—or at least that wasn't the kind of astrology I was interested in. I wanted to learn how to feel comfortable counseling someone about the future.

I started working with the crop theory—of using a ten degree orb on any transiting planet that was applying in a hard aspect. The hard aspects have a greater chance at altering the personality; they bring more energy than the soft ones; they could enhance a greater growth possibility. Because the Sun, Moon and Mercury move so quickly, I didn't feel they would be particularly helpful in the process of individuation. Venus, too, stayed too close to the Sun to really do more than reflect the mood of the moment.

Mars brought anger with it. People did rash things on a Mars transit. What about transforming the energy? Various philosophies teach the conversion of anger into creativity—the alchemy of personality. Mars energy could be rechanneled. In order to begin the process of developing creativity, in order to further the process of individuation, the Mars anger would have to become productive. The work of Dr. Heber J. Smith, made available to members of the American Federation of Astrologers, was very helpful when I was looking for clues as to how to get this process in motion. (His work was presented in manuscript form. It was called Transits. It is still available from the AFA.)

It was difficult to learn how to transform the Mars energy for it activates the chart in such a way that it's easy to get caught up in the energy flow. The attempt to transform this energy was discussed with all my friends and they got copies of their Mars transit energies, too. I needed feedback. Then my students and clients started working with the transformation of Mars energy, and they found the transcendental experience exciting.

We then moved into a ten degree orb for the slow moving planets. Jupiter brought about two months of pressure, Saturn a year, Uranus two, and Neptune and Pluto hit for about five. This gives us plenty of time to work with what these transits represent. We have a chance to understand them. We can begin to utilize the concept symbolized by the transit. Instead of becoming the victim of a transit, we can work with the higher side of the energy. We have a chance to grow. We have the opportunity to read the signs along the road and make adjustments in our lives.

Some astrologers were afraid of a Saturn transit, often assuming that any transit of Saturn would bring some loss or restriction with it. But Saturn also symbolizes the crystalization process. It symbolizes responsibility. Looking at a Saturn transit from that point, it began to indicate a period of maturation. A Saturn transit was similar to taking a mid-term exam in the school of life. It was saying, "How much do you know?" It was saying, "Based on your age and experience, your Sun sign and your needs at this point in time, how are you going to handle yourself?" This is Saturn as the teacher, the tester.

The hero's venture, or the process of individuation, is one that requires that we be tested. When an American Indian wished to become a warrior for the tribe, he was sent into the wilderness to be tested. Our life experiences and reactions are tested, too, and the Saturn transits test the various facets of our personality in order that we become conscious of what we know. And that process takes about a year. We cannot determine how we are doing when the transit is observed using a three degree orb, because by that time, the test is over and the results are coming in.

Using a ten degree orb (applying only), the planet's energy begins to manifest, it builds in strength, it tells you what has to be learned, it gives us a chance to learn the material, and then the pressure is off. The pressure of any transit is the most intense about three degrees away from the exact aspect (conjunction, square or opposition). By the time the transit has become exact, the pressure is gone, and as the transit moves away from the natal planet, its effect is dispersed. Hopefully it leaves us more wise, more mature, more comfortable being us.

The system can be helpful if one is interested in making life easier. It works very well if one is interested in becoming self responsible. For those who want to work with understanding the natal chart, the transits tell you which part of personality is up for growing now. This system gives us advance notice about our lives, what needs to be learned, what the changes are all about. We don't experience life for nothing—life is not just an accident. It can be a process of becoming aware.

The transit system allows us to become our own counselors. It helps us learn how to advise ourselves. Before we can do that, however, we must become familiar with the system, and we have to let go of the human tendency to approach the future with fear or apprehension. Transits also have to be viewed according to one's age, for a twenty-year-old will respond differently than a fifty-year-old.

Students just beginning to work with the transit system can read for others, but when it comes to themselves, they tend to view upcoming changes with too much gloom and doom. As they become more familiar with the theory, they can begin to trust the universe more. We are not born to be hurt, we are not born to lose. We are born to work with what we have.

This book is not meant to provide all the answers. Some transits may not even be completely covered, because most of the material has been compiled from classes—and sometimes we just couldn't think of all the ramifications of a transit. This material will hopefully help you begin to ask the right questions.

Part 1

Transits
of the Planets

Sun Transits

I don't work with the transits of the Sun to the natal planets in the chart. The Sun's influence is fleeting and the concentration of energy involved in diagnosing its transits will keep the mind preoccupied with small details rather than attempting to throw the consciousness into a greater and more general plan. People who watch Sun transits are somewhat akin to those who look for cracks in the sidewalk—they miss the tall buildings, the wonderful architecture, the warmth of the Sun and the beautiful mountain in the distance.

However, one transiting aspect worth observing is the Sun's annual cycle. On your birthday, the transiting Sun conjuncts your natal Sun. The week before and after your birthday is often a depressing period, for the inner self is evaluating the past year. The birthday period could be interpreted as each person's "New Year." Pagans of yore noticed that the spirit was at a low ebb during the birthday time, so birthday presents and festivities would cheer the heart and encourage us to keep on living and growing. It's important that we celebrate our day doing something we like.

When the Sun opposes your natal Sun you are in a secondary depression, as the year is now half over. Each quarter period, when the transiting Sun squares your natal Sun, indicates a minor low. The importance of observing this yearly cycle by transit manifests when you are planning your work load. It's wise to take better care of yourself during these periods, to maintain a good diet, to allow for enough sleep, to avoid a strenuous vacation or an extra heavy work schedule. If proper nourishment and care is not provided for the body, the tendency to catch a cold, the flu or a virus is more prevalent. Obviously we will out-live our Sun transits! But we can maintain better health if we notice when these periods occur each year.

Moon Transits

In the process of becoming conscious or self aware, the transiting Moon will not have a great affect either. The Moon changes signs every two and a half days. It will conjunct, square or oppose something in your chart frequently. The transiting Moon is better used to diagnose mundane events. In C.C. Zain's *Horary Astrology* published by the Church of Light, the signs and aspects of the Moon are discussed so they can be used when planning successful events. I recommend that a client use Moon transits only if he has a history of extreme behavior during full Moon periods.

The Moon is an indicator of the mood of the masses. It rules the tides and functions on a twenty-eight day cycle that also relates to the female menstrual cycle. The Moon symbolizes the material manifestation of gestation on the Earth. Moon transits don't help us solve long term personal problems or change our lives on deep inner levels so they are better used to indicate a mood.

Mercury Transits

Mercury also moves too quickly to be of use except as it goes retrograde or direct. When Mercury is moving in a forward motion, communication seems to go better; people seem to understand each other; plans are made easily. Mercury moods reflect the sign it's in at the moment. For example, when Mercury is transiting through the sign of Aries, people are more outspoken and direct; when transiting the sign of Cancer, people talk of love, romance, nurturing, and they may be more emotional about words.

When Mercury goes retrograde, or apparently moves backward in the zodiac, communication becomes muddled, directions are misunderstood, plans go awry, letters are written in haste, letters that are mailed don't arrive at the proper destination, traffic is snarled, contracts misunderstood, many petty misunderstandings take place. Knowing when Mercury goes retrograde can help you to avoid some of these entanglements. When we are aware of the potential misunderstandings, we can allow more time for travel, as well as allowing for the inevitable misunderstandings.

Mercury also reflects the mood of the crowd much like the Moon. It can be considered when planning events.

Venus Transits

Venus moves very quickly in the zodiac, never being too far from the Sun. Like Mercury, its effect is fleeting and it can be used to indicate a good day, a minor upset or a minor blessing. Unless it retrogrades and stays in a ten degree applying orb to an important configuration in your chart at a crucial time in your life, it's not worth charting or worrying about. You can quickly scan the ephemeris and note where Venus gets stuck for a few weeks. The effect of Venus will not be devastating.

Mars Transits

Mars represents the action principle in the natal horoscope. It has been blamed for anger and violence and even war. The action principle reflects our energy potential. The Mars position in the chart indicates how we personally take action. It indicates how we will *act out our Sun energy* as well as how we act in a career sense, how we act around our friends, how we love, what our sex drive is all about. Because Mars indicates sexuality, it symbolizes the life force within each of us. A Mars transit symbolizes the energy in the universe, the action energy, the life energy, the sexual energy, the libido.

As Mars conjuncts, squares or opposes any of our natal planets, it brings energy and life to the facets of personality that are symbolized by those planets. The sextile and trine bring effortless energy while the hard aspects bring energy that needs to be refocused or rechanneled so that it can become productive or constructive.

Reprogramming sexual energy is the beginning of the creative experience. As we learn to reprogram our creative energy, the anger shown by the previously unchanneled energy will disappear, and the constructive activities can emerge. If we ever wish to be in command of our ship we need to take responsibility for handing our energy in a mature fashion. It's easy to learn. Remember, use a ten degree applying orb.

The following section includes some "cookbook" interpretations of how this energy can manifest in the chart. Obviously, the less productive forms of the energy could be reprogrammed into more productive ones! If we can look back at our charts and plot our less pleasant behavior according to our Mars transits, then we are not really in command of our ship. I have found that any attempt to change these transiting effects helps us grow more aware. The energy is thrown at us, much like someone throws a "hot potato." If we just step aside and let the hot potato fall unnoticed, we have at least made a step in the direction toward self-responsibility.

• Mars conjunct, square or opposing natal Sun

High Energy. The accent is on the self. This period brings a lot of energy with it, but we may become so tremendously energetic that we over-work, over-play or get just plain accident prone because we're in too much of a hurry. We can be more easily angered during this period, and when feelings are hurt, we may get a cold or the flu or some kind of virus. This period needs watching as far as career/business moves are concerned. It is colored by the aspects to the natal Sun: if the Sun carries hard aspects in the natal chart, the Mars transit will energize those aspects. In this case, the transit will indicate a time to use caution, to make some attempt to control how we react under pressure.

• Mars conjunct, square or opposing natal Moon

Supersensitive. This is the roughest Mars transit possible in the chart. The Moon represents our emotional responses, how we feel, how we respond to life around us. The Mars transit combines anger with the feeling responses, often resulting in a super-sensitive reaction to all that is going on around us. We are highly sensitive, overly emotional, often angry. Any suggestions made regarding either personal life or career may be misinterpreted as some form of criticism. The emotional rug can be easily pulled out from under us and we may feel ourselves reacting in an extremely emotional manner to situations that would have made us smile a week before the transit came in. Most of the hurt feelings are in our heads; we may be wearing our hearts on our sleeves and rubbing elbows in the crowd! This is not the time to make major decisions regarding either love or work, as we are just plain mad. We can be accident prone, so drive more carefully. Anger can be worked out through physical labor.

This cycle really used to "get" me. I had fights with my friends, fellow employees and loved ones. I was so emotionally upset that I could rarely get any work done. By learning how to rechannel this energy, this cycle became my most productive! It is difficult to reprogram but it can be done. The anger will evaporate and it can be expended somewhere. So, I washed windows, scrubbed and waxed floors, and for a while I had the shiniest apartment in New York City. The first few minutes of planned labor were difficult because I tried to procrastinate—just one more cigarette, just one more phone call, etc. But when the work started, all the anger went out on the floor or the windows, or in painting the living room walls! Now I don't need to do that anymore, and when an article needs to be written, or some work has to be accomplished, this transit can be used in a highly productive manner.

• *Mars conjunct square or opposing natal Mercury*

Talk Too Much. Mars is the action planet and when it aspects natal Mercury (ruling the mind, the speech, sight, hearing, etc.), it activates our mouths and ears. When this happens we have a tendency to be careless about what we say; we may misinterpret what we hear; we may write letters that are very unclear. Mars energy is speeding up the brain, so to speak! We tend to make the assumption that people understand more than they can; we may assume that people are more competent than they are. This is a period when orders and contracts are written in a vague fashion and instructions are misinterpreted. Supervisors misunderstand employees and vice versa—communication is jumbled. We can avoid silly misunderstandings by using some extra caution.

Because the mind is functioning so quickly, hasty and angry letters can be written. If you have a score to settle, do it later when you will be more rational. And because the brain waves are functioning so quickly, its easy to jump over the important parts of contracts you sign. Not only should you look at the small print, but try the large type as well—little things like due dates, complete costs, or when the production is scheduled to go into action!

Communication becomes difficult. When Mercury is retrograde by transit, everyone has trouble getting information straight. But when Mars is aspecting your natal Mercury by transit, you are the person who seems to misunderstand everything. Either you are talking so quickly that your point is missed completely, or you are in such a hurry that you don't hear what others are saying to you. If a relationship is important to you, this is the time to say, "I beg your pardon? I didn't understand what you said." And rather than becoming angry because your partner didn't hear you correctly the first time around, be ready to repeat yourself. Be ready to ask others to repeat themselves in order to ascertain that you heard correctly what was being said. These aspects take place several times a year. They happen to you and they happen to the person you love at different times. When you understand this energy, you won't let it be the beginning of the end of a relationship for those misunderstandings won't take place.

The most humorous part of this transit is the silly misunderstandings that happen because you think you are "smarter" than anyone you know at the moment. It's funny because the mind is functioning so quickly that most people around you can't keep up with your train of thought. Therefore loved ones, working partners, fellow employees all become exasperatingly slow. Remember, they get this cycle a couple of times a year, too, and they may feel the same way about you!

• Mars conjunct, square or opposing natal Venus

In Love with Love/Vacation. In the natal chart, Venus represents what we desire, what we want around us in terms of entertainment and fun, as well as what kind of a love relationship we are looking for. The Venus definition of love is an intellectual concept rather than a physical reality, so it can be descriptive of what we want from love in a highly idealized sense.

The transit of Mars to natal Venus will push your emotional nature to the front. It brings out the romantic in each of us. We all need the candlelight dinner, romancing and dancing, love and affection at this time of the year. If you have already found someone to love, this is a time to express that love, to do some courting and romancing. If you are looking for someone, this may be a period when you look too hard. As my mother used to say, "You have fallen in love with love!" You may push an ultimatum on a new relationship long before you should bring up such matters—such as "Marry me or else." Or you may just fall in love with love and put those feelings of love on some unworthy person. Mother also said, "Don't make love by the garden gate, 'cause love is blind but the neighbors ain't!" Which is a country way of saying be careful—but it took me years to understand what she meant. I thought she meant that I should be more discrete about being affectionate in public! However, she meant that the neighbors (or other people in general) can see what you can't—they can see that you picked a person who is not your peer, or a person who is not as interested in you as you may be in him, etc. This is a great transit for making poor judgements.

One of my clients reported back to me that she really made a fool out of herself on this one. Before she knew what she was doing, she had pushed an ultimatum on her new boyfriend—she wanted to live with him with an eye for getting married, and decided to talk to him about it rather forcefully. They had only been dating about five weeks, and the gentleman in question told her that he felt he was being pushed, that he was not ready to make that kind of a commitment, that he didn't know her well enough. And he was right. After Mars went off her Venus she knew he was right, but in the meantime the budding relationship had ended. She did have a sense of humor about it however, and resolved to be a bit more careful on the next one.

Because Mars transits to the natal Venus also involve pleasure, it might be a good time to take a vacation. Venus indicates our particular enjoyments and we especially enjoy having fun during this transit. Our enjoyment may be restricted by the other aspects to Venus indicated in the natal chart, but if we understand how those aspects work, we can keep a healthy perspective on the energy we have going for us.

For example, if Venus conjuncts Saturn natally, and the Mars transit is activating both planets at the same time, both energies will be felt. When you check the Mars-Saturn transits you'll discover that it brings delays. In regard to a vacation, knowing the delay-restriction factor, it's easy to plan ahead, allowing plenty of time for any possible delay. During this time you may want to avoid the necessity of inter-connecting flights, for example, thereby keeping the vacation enjoy-able.

Should Venus be in hard aspect to Jupiter natally, this transit will combine the Venus function with that of Jupiter, and this individual may over-spend during this transit. The vacation can still be enjoyed, especially if it is purchased ahead of time—for that will keep the Jupiterian spending within bounds.

• *Mars conjunct, square or opposing natal Jupiter*

Bad Buying Cycle. This transit influences our buying power. Magnets reach out from store windows and tempt us to buy something we don't need. When we make major purchases during this period, we either buy something that we don't need or we pay too much for what we get. If we buy equipment we may get the "lemon" variety. This is not the time to buy a house or to rent an apartment. It's not the time to buy a new car unless you like large mechanic bills. Being a skeptic, I bought my first car on this transit, testing the theory. The car was new and it was towed from a legal parking spot one hour after buying it! There were six different addresses on the parking ticket when I finally saw it at the police pound. I came out of the house with a friend to look for my car and a trailer truck was parked where it had been. I was looking under the truck, despairing about the possibility of my new car being stolen, when a man on the street approached us and asked if we were looking for a little yellow car. He told us it had just been towed away by the police.

The first tank of gas I purchased was full of water. Thank heaven the car didn't have power steering like the other cars on the highway that had been filled with watered-down gas. There was a complete blockup on the Connecticut Turnpike that night. My car hobbled over to the shoulder of the road and was safe but the cars with power steering stopped dead when the watered-down gas hit their engines and there were so many accidents that cars spilled over all the lanes of the highway. It took me eleven hours to get from Darien, Connecticut to the Bronx in New York where the car finally died. I put in a new battery, a new fuel pump and a new gas tank. From then on, the car was a mess—for every time the transit of Mars hit my Jupiter the car was back in the garage, or disabled on the highway with some major problem.

I shopped for my next car during the same cycle! I didn't buy it then, but I decided to buy it on a Mars-Jupiter transit. And of course that car cost me more than the first one did. Clients with lemons began to check when they made the purchase and reported back to me that their lemons were purchased or looked at under the Mars-Jupiter affliction.

People in the business of buying merchandise often over-buy

during this cycle—they overstock their stores or expend huge amounts of unnecessary money. Items bought on sale during this period are often unsatisfactory later. People who buy homes pay too much for what they get, and people who are renting apartments usually find some lovely over-priced place to live and can't afford to keep it without becoming rent poor.

Relationships can be affected by this cycle as well. Jupiter in the natal chart reflects how we relate to others, how we open up or expand. When Mars comes along by transit, it gives our relating ability some incentive, and the tendency is to overreact, overrespond. People say, "I don't care, I want it anyway," or "I don't care, I'll do it anyway." The future is forgotten and the immediate need of the moment is the only one that's important. She wants to go out to dinner and he doesn't—so she says, "I don't care what you want to do, I'm going." When we start thinking "I don't care," we're getting ready to go down the wrong path. This energy should be curbed; the period can be lived through, and finances can be carefully held at bay. When the transit is over, we have some money in our pockets, we don't have a pile of unwanted clothes or appliances, and we can make better buying decisions.

• Mars conjunct, square or opposing natal Saturn

Problems With Men, Authority Figures, Legal Matters. When Mars transits the natal Saturn position, it brings to life the restrictions, cautions, and internal authority problems we may need to work free. It also indicates difficulty when we attempt to communicate with the men in our lives. If you are a man, and need to get permission from a fellow employee (male) you may have difficulty with him. If the decision is an important one, you may be wise to let it lay until the transit is no longer in effect.

A woman with this transit is apt to find her male friends more difficult than usual. She may want to talk to a man, to discuss certain aspects of her life—her plans, her hopes—during this period, or she may just want to socialize. And the men in her life won't respond well. It's pointless to have a fight with your husband or to break up with a boyfriend on this one, for it happens two or three times a year and needs to be handled by other methods.

Authority figures present a problem, perhaps because our "caution point" has been activated, and our inner attitude may be responsible for the lousy response we get. The transit brings good ideas with it, but because we are "right" we may proceed in the situation somewhat akin to a Sherman tank, proving to those around us how right we are, and they don't listen anyway. Good suggestions, permissions that are needed, and situations of a similar nature will not go well during this period. An authority figure during this transit may be anything or anyone thwarting our progress. So busses run late, we run into traffic jams, planes and trains aren't on time, inter-connecting flights don't connect. Knowing these possibilities exist, it's wise to leave a little early, allow extra time to avoid the frustration.

Legal matters usually don't have a healthy outcome if started under this transit. Any situation involving "red tape" will be delayed in some way. If it's possible, handle the legality before the transit begins or after it has ended.

Example: Back to my car again! When I sold my car it had Vermont plates on it, and I sold it in New York state. I had to keep a copy of the registration according to Vermont state law. In New York state you get a duplicate registration to give to the new owner so he can re-register the car in his name, but in Vermont you don't. I called the Vermont Department of Motor Vehicles (not a big deal, eh?) to get a duplicate registration. And Mars hit the tenth degree before it was to conjunct natal Saturn. And the duplicate never came. The man who bought the car called every day—the deal wasn't finalized until he got his registration, so I had his money but he couldn't drive or even register his car. The day that Mars went off my Saturn the registration form came! Not a big delay, and not even something I needed for myself, but nevertheless a delay. Students applying for loans at school, people needing official permissions, run into restrictions and delays during this period. It can be most frustrating!

The most important thing to avoid during this transit is the tendency toward "righteousness" that we can so easily develop. Because we are right, because we have a good idea, we tend to present that idea in a very high-handed manner. This alienates those who would otherwise be helpful. Write down the good ideas and save them for presentation when the transit is over—then your good ideas will be accepted. It takes the crystallization process involving natal Saturn to turn the idea into something you can talk about. The transit isn't all bad.

• *Mars conjunct, square or opposing natal Uranus*

Super Impulsive. This is an impetuous transit for it activates natal Uranus, bringing emphasis and energy to the part of us that symbolizes eccentricity. If Uranus describes eccentricity, individualistic behavior, the part of us that is stubborn or willful, then the Mars transit to it indicates a period when caution needs to be exercised. The transit causes a tendency to throw caution to the winds; we forget about tomorrow or next week, or what might be good for us next year. Long range plans are thrown out of the window as we look for immediate satisfaction or the good feeling of an immediate temper tantrum.

This period can be handled better by exercising some thought — will the party we're going to tonight cause us to lose our job tomorrow because we won't be able to make that important meeting? Are we hitchhiking on a public highway today really to save bus fare — or does it bespeak of an urge to "go out of control" and put us in a vulnerable position? Keep in mind that life is much like a game of chess — every move we make reflects the position of our king.

One should keep in mind the natal position of Uranus when reading this transit — what house it's in, and what natal aspects are made to it. If Uranus squares your natal Moon, the transit will be harder to live with than if it remains unaspected in the fourth house.

• *Mars conjunct, square or opposing natal Neptune*

Perception Loss. This one is fun because it indicates a time in life when we don't really know what we are doing. We may have problems navigating around furniture in the house or office. A friend of mine sideswiped several cars on an empty street early in the morning while under this transit. Normally she was a good driver. She said she was completely sober, but she didn't think her car took up that much space! No major damage was done, but she was plenty embarrassed.

This is a time when gossip can be turned against us, so avoid the office gossip and avoid the family "did you hears" if at all possible. We may not react normally: there is a tendency to go off diets, or to crave foods and alcoholic beverages more than usual—and we may not handle drugs or alcohol in our normal fashion. Someone who normally has two drinks before dinner may become tipsy over one glass of wine.

This is a period when we may be able to better tune into our dreams, goals or aspirations. We may be more gullible, too. It is a good time for meditation, yoga or spiritual work for the mind is ready to respond to a higher vibration.

• *Mars conjunct, square or opposing natal Pluto*

Anger. This one activates an anger period for it stirs memories in the unconscious and makes us feel more gullible. Pluto indicates the unconscious motivation within us—the memories of early childhood experience that we might want to forget. Pluto can bring to light some of our "control" needs. When Mars activates this point by transit, we may feel a bit out of control, and therefore edgy. A chance word overheard can make us angry or hurt and in spite of the conscious self, we wind up being angry.

Because Mars activates parts of the unconscious, this can be an excellent period for those who wish to become more aware of the sensitive aspects of personality. It could be that parents laughed at us over some sensitive issue and the memory is buried. Along comes Mars and we get angry over a slight that reminds us of an old incident we thought was long forgotten. Evidently, it's important. The memory can be consciously analyzed in terms of our present needs. What do we need? What are we so sensitive about? If it's a legitimate sensitivity it needs to be acknowleged. Each person has different needs, and all too often we tend to suppress those personal needs and sensitivities.

It's important to acknowlege Pluto's aspects in the natal chart, for the Mars energy will activate any natal aspect. This could be a period when we draw unhealthy situations to us, or we participate in unhealthy activities that concern the lower forms of Pluto energy. If this is the case, and we are trying to re-channel this natal aspect, this is a time to stay home and out of trouble.

For example, a young client had a Mars-Pluto opposition involving her natal Moon. During the transiting Mars periods, she would go out and drink too much. After becoming drunk, she would pick up strangers in bars. The next morning brought terrible feelings of guilt and self-hate. During the process of trying to understand what caused this kind of behavior, she also began to avoid the bar scene when the transit hit. Because she kept a diary we were able to pinpoint her periods of irresponsible behavior. Avoiding these unattractive experiences made her feel much more comfortable with herself.

• *Mars transiting the angles of the natal chart*

Mars transits will activate the angles of the chart and emphasize certain life action.

First House. When Mars goes over the Ascendant (actually ten degrees before it reaches the Ascendant), it will activate the matters of the first house. This is an excellent time to "put yourself out there" for this energy can be used to develop career matters or your social life or both. Even if you aren't feeling well, even if you are feeling antisocial, the transit can be used for good purpose. You can't make those contacts sitting at home in your closet, so get out there and respond to your own personal energy cycle!

Fourth House. When Mars gets ten degrees away from the fourth house cusp, it activates the home front. Either you'll entertain a lot, or get into cleaning and redecorating your home or apartment. You'll be thinking about moving, or you'll be thinking about changing your home. This energy doesn't guarantee a move, but a change or a desire to change.

Seventh House. When Mars gets ten degrees away from your seventh house cusp, it will start to activate seventh house matters. People you know socially, as well as marriage or business partners, will be making demands on your time. This may not involve work—it may mean that everyone you know is asking you to dinner, to join them in some activity *they* enjoy. After several days of this kind of attention, some of us begin to feel resentful—for we are not getting our work done. And we are not being asked if *we* really want to do any of this stuff. Keep the peace, for the energy only lasts for a couple of weeks!

Tenth House. When Mars gets ten degrees away from the tenth house cusp, the career is activated. If you work, the office will be superbusy and it's not a time to plan a vacation. You need to keep in touch with what's going on. If you don't work, matters that affect your public image or the volunteer work that you do will need your help and attention. It's time to get out there and do it.

• *Planning your Mars Potential*

Mars spends about two years going through all the signs in the zodiac. This means that Mars will make a hard aspect to each of your planets two or three times in the space of a year. As Mars moves to zero degrees of the Cardinal signs, it's getting ready to set off problems associated with any planets you have in Cardinal signs. (They are Aries, Cancer, Libra, Capricorn.) As Mars begins to move into a Fixed sign, look for action involving planets in the signs Taurus, Leo, Scorpio or Aquarius. As it moves into the Mutable signs, Mars will activate any planet in Gemini, Virgo, Sagittarius or Pisces. We can make a list of the energy type and the time of year that this energy will manifest.

For those readers who are students of astrology, this section is written to help you get started plotting the Mars transit. If you are an advanced student and fully understand the mathematic principles involved in locating transits in an ephemeris, you don't need to read this section.

Using sample chart "A" we can begin to plot the Mars cycles. Because this chart belongs to a client it has not been identified. It belongs to a young woman who works in a posh mid-town New York publishing house. She has a great deal of responsibility and tends to overwork. She wants to learn how to best use her energy. Her responsibilities include raising a child and caring for the man she lives with. In order to make the most productive use of her time, learning how to handle the Mars transits will help her plan her schedule. This way she will be able to accomplish as much as possible in the least amount of time.

Publishing several trade journals a month doesn't allow much time for "wallowing" in personal misunderstandings. If she wishes to be a good mother, she can't require that her child suffer during her overly sensitive periods. In order to maintain a sense of herself amidst her pressures, she can plot the Mars cycles and be prepared for the rough ones, relaxing on the easier ones. There are periods when Mars is quiet, making no hard aspects to her chart, and requiring little attention. These are the best times for social activities or taking time out for just

CHART A

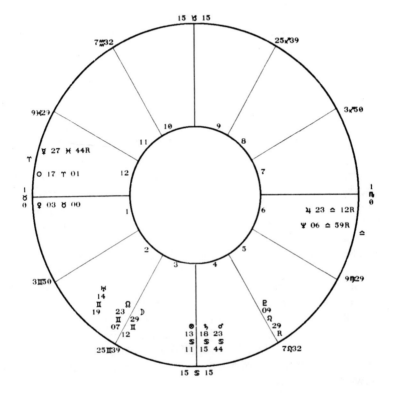

plain fun. When the hard aspects are in effect, they create tensions that can be re-channeled into getting rid of a complicated work load. As you watch how we plot the aspects in her chart, you can learn to do your own.

Get an ephemeris that covers 1979, 1980 and 1981 so you can follow along with me. On January 1, 1980, Mars is at 13° Virgo. If you look at the natal chart included here, you'll see that natal Uranus is at 14° of Gemini, and transiting Mars is squaring it. If you turn back to December of 1979, you'll see that Mars in transit is still in the sign of Virgo, and turning back to November of 1979 you'll see that Mars hits 4° Virgo on November 30th. Using a ten degree applying orb, Mars began to square her natal Uranus on November 30, 1979. It continues to square natal Uranus during the whole month of December and the transit becomes exact on January 8, 1980. Mars then retrogrades back to 14° Virgo on January 25, 1980 and remains in orb until February 29, 1980 when it hits 4° Virgo again. It retrogrades back into the sign of Leo during March, April and May. On May 17, 1980 Mars hits 4° Virgo again and is in orb to square her natal Uranus until June 11, 1980.

Her natal Moon is at 29° Gemini and natal Mercury is at 27° Pisces—both Mutable signs. Mars in Virgo by transit will square the Moon and oppose Mercury. It also sets off a natal square between the two. By nature, she finds it difficult to communicate (Mercury) her feelings (Moon). Because Mercury is in the twelfth house, she keeps her problems to herself, and often doesn't discuss emotional problems until she's solved them. These natal difficulties will be set off while Mars (by transit) heats up the natal square. The transit will also activate the problems mentioned previously in the section on Mars-Moon and Mars-Mercury. We can safely say, then, that this will be a sensitive period for job, personal life, as well as husband and child relationships. The tension starts to build on June 16, 1980 when Mars hits 17° of Virgo (ten degrees away from an opposition to her natal Mercury). It stays in orb, growing in intensity until July 10th.

Mars is now heading for the Cardinal sign of Libra, getting ready to activate her natal Neptune, Sun, Saturn, Mars and Jupiter! On July 6, 1980, Mars hits 27° Virgo (ten degrees away from her 7° Libra Neptune). It stays in orb until July 24th. Neptune squares the Moon natally, so not only does she suffer from the perceptual distortions described in the Mars-Neptune section, but the transit activates the natal square. There is a wide opposition involving the Sun as well. This may indicate a period when anger and a loss of perception, a preoccupation with fantasy, drugs, alcohol or delusions will color decisions she may make. These decisions will relate to her emotional needs (Moon) or her spiritual needs (Sun). Because she knows what's coming, she can be more aware—she can avoid major decisions regarding emotional or spiritual things until her head is clear. Or she can slow down and think more carefully. The Neptune-Mars transit might indicate a good period for mediation and yoga—to help pull her energy inward, so it can be rechanneled into a more constructive direction.

Mars hits 6° Libra on July 22, 1980 and sets off a natal t-square. The Sun at 16° Aries opposes Jupiter at 23° Libra, and both planets square Mars conjunct Saturn in Cancer at 18° and 23° respectively. The tension builds until August 19, 1980. She will learn how to cope with a combination of unpleasant situations. Mars opposing her Sun by transit brings lots of energy and drive. Mars squaring Saturn by transit indicates problems discussing situations with men in general, her husband in particular, authority figures of any sort. The transiting Mars conjuncts natal Jupiter at the same time bringing on an urge for impulse buying, overpaying and a generally bad attitude as far as relationships are concerned.

The transit sets off the natal aspects as well so it becomes a tense period. The natal frustration caused by Saturn/Mars square the Sun will be activated. The Jupiter opposition to her Sun indicates that she is not used to relating to her own needs—and Jupiter squaring Mars/Saturn indicates that she doesn't relate easily to men or to authority figures. There is a chance that she may give up needs of her own in order to maintain a sexual or love relationship. She will have to cope with a tendency to act in a self-destructive manner symbolized by Mars square the Sun in the natal chart. In keywords this reads, "I act (Mars) against (the square) my spiritual self (the Sun) or the "I am" principle as some people call it. This self-destructive tendency does not mean that she will kill herself—it means that she may cut her nose off to spite her face!

Saturn square the Sun natally indicates a difficulty with the father image, perhaps a basic resentment or fear of those in authority. The aspect may promote apprehension about authority, or an assumption that all authority figures will disapprove of what she does. This aspect sometimes causes a great deal of frustration or a suppression of anger—for the attitude may be coming from unconscious childhood memories that have been long repressed or forgotten.

Jupiter opposing the Sun in the natal chart also indicates that she doesn't relate to her own needs by nature. As a child she may have been taught that her personal needs are not important—or that "woman" needs aren't important. She tends to give up her "self" in order to complete a relationship, not realizing that the guy would probably relate to her needs or go along with them if she would only let him know what they are.

All these natal tensions are operating along with the additional tension caused by the Mars transit. This period (July 22 through August 19, 1980) will be a hard one to get through—but she's done it before because it hits several times a year anyway. The re-channeling of energy will probably not be accomplished in the first go round of handling this transit consciously, but some constructive dents can be made in the problem.

Don't be afraid to tell people about transit pressures; chances are they were alive before you met them and they survived these transits before you talked to them. Anything you say will make a transit like this easier to handle—not harder. The energy begins to manifest when Mars first approaches the ten degree orb, the tension builds as Mars gets closer and closer to the exact aspect, and the tension is gone when Mars reaches the exact conjunction, square or opposition.

Each successive pass of Mars over the Cardinal signs will help this lady understand how the energy works within her, and she'll get ideas as to how she can use it better. Eventually, after working on becoming conscious of this kind of energy, she may find this to be one of her most productive periods.

On August 18, 1980, Mars by transit is at 22° Libra and ten degrees away from an oppostion to natal Venus at 2° Taurus. So from August 18 until September 2, 1980, she'll feel the pressure of the Mars-Venus opposition, activating the conditions discussed under that aspect. She has a natal square between Venus and Pluto and that natal aspect will be activated at the same time.

From August 29th until September 13, 1980, transiting Mars will square natal Pluto, causing the Venus-Pluto square to remain active, as well as introducing an element of anger that comes from an unconscious source. She may be overly sensitive to ideas about knowing where she stands in her love relationship during this period. She may unconsciously become manipulative and this may cause resentment to be directed at her.

Nothing happens in the chart until October 18th when Mars by transit hits 4° Sagittarius and begins to oppose natal Uranus again. And the pattern repeats itself. Each round of Mars gives us an opportunity to look at ourselves and to begin re-channeling the raw energy. As we polish it, we grow more productive and less unhappy.

The cycles repeat for the next year and a half as follows:

High Energy (Mars conjunct, square or opposing natal Sun)
Dec. 1 - Dec. 23, 1980
March 25 - April 17, 1981
July 28 - August 23, 1981
Super-Sensitive (Mars conjunct, square or opposing natal Moon)
Nov. 5 - Nov. 22, 1980
Mar. 1 - Mar. 17, 1981
June 30 - July 18, 1981
Nov. 21 - Dec. 15, 1981
Talk-too-Much (Mars conjunct, square or opposing natal Mercury)
Nov. 5 - Nov. 22, 1980
Mar. 1 - Mar. 17, 1980
June 30 - July 18, 1981
Nov. 21 - Dec. 15, 1981
In Love with Love (Mars conjunct, square or opposing natal Venus)
Dec. 21, 1980 - Jan. 3, 1981
April 15 - April 29, 1981
Aug. 21 - Sept. 6, 1981
Bad Buying Cycle (Mars conjunct, square or opposing natal Jupiter)
Dec. 1 - Dec. 23, 1980
Mar. 25 - April 17, 1981
July 28 - Aug. 23, 1981
Problems with Authority/Men (Mars conjunct, square or opposing natal Saturn)
Dec. 1 - Dec. 23, 1980
March 25 - April 17, 1981
July 28 - Aug. 23, 1981
Super-Impulsive (Mars conjunct, square or opposing natal Uranus)
Oct. 18 - Nov. 1, 1980
Feb. 12 - Feb. 26, 1981
June 11 - June 26, 1981
Oct. 28 - Nov. 16, 1981;

Loss of Perception/Meditation (Mars conjunct, square or opposing natal Neptune)
Nov. 19 - Dec. 2, 1980
March 14 - March 27, 1981
July 14 - July 30, 1981
Dec. 10, 1981 - Jan. 2, 1982
Unconscious Angers (Mars conjunct, square or opposing natal Pluto)
Dec. 30, 1980 - Jan. 12, 1981
April 24 - May 8, 1981
Sept. 1 - Sept. 17, 1981

You will note that some transits occur simultaneously. For example, Mars by transit hits the Sun, Mars, Saturn and Jupiter during the same period in this chart. These periods have been separated on the list above. When several transits happen at one time it's wise to inform clients of the overlapping energy, to make sure that each person understands the kind of pressure he's under and how much pressure he's under. If you glibly lump all the transits together, it doesn't sound so hard. It may become more frustrating for the client when he attempts to control this energy.

A Mars to Mars cycle has not been included in this section. Mars transiting its natal position is really a cycle and not a transit. If you are interested in a common-sense approach to cycles, a book is forthcoming! If you can't wait for mine, you may like to investigate a fairly new publication, *Cycles of Becoming* by Alexander Ruperti, published by CRCS Publications.

Looking at the chart of a man (Chart B) we see the Mars energy manifest a little differently. I have deliberately chosen the chart of another Cardinal sign person, so you can see that all Cardinal signs will not be affected in the same manner. This young man is in the middle of a crisis caused by pressure to change his career. He has mentioned also that he feels tremendous internal pressure from time to time, and much of the internal pressure may be activated as Mars transits his natal planets.

On January 1, 1980, transiting Mars is in Virgo. When you look at his chart, you'll notice several planets in Mutable signs, and the closest one to transiting Mars is his natal Saturn. Going back to 1979, you'll begin to see where the transit starts. Because Mars is going retrograde

CHART B

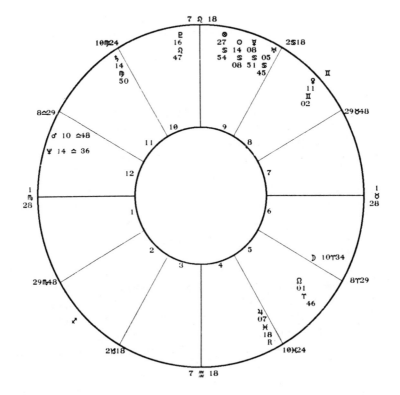

in 1980, you might want to go back into 1979 so that you can give him a better picture of just when this difficult time started to manifest.

He has Saturn at 14° Virgo, Venus at 11° Gemini, and Jupiter at 7° Pisces. As long as Mars is in a Mutable sign, these planets will be energized by the transit. November and December of 1979 were tense months because all three of his Mutable planets were being energized and this energy also activates a t-square in his natal chart.

Looking at the natal Venus, we see that he is fond of controversy (Gemini) and that it is difficult for him to express his feelings of love and affection because Venus is blocked by both Saturn and Jupiter. The square from Venus to Saturn indicates that his parents didn't set a really good image for him to follow in regard to loving someone. When he reaches out to seek love, the Saturn (or some psychological block effected by his father in his early life) restricts that ability. Because Jupiter also blocks Venus, he may over-and underrelate to what he loves and this can cause a love/hate polarity about his desires in life. These desires range from his love of a woman to his love of his work. He can be moody and temperamental at the same time he feels blocked and restricted. His expectancy factor is low, for the Saturn-Venus square did not encourage him to expect much when he was a child. When Mars by transit comes along to activate this personality factor, he feels the natal aspects along with the impetus to express the energy discussed in the sections about Mars/Venus, Mars/Jupiter and Mars/Saturn.

During November and December of 1979, up until the Spring of 1980, he will be coping with a great deal of tension. He wants to romance and play (Venus) but he feels restricted because of Saturn and he may wish to "chuck it all" because the Jupiter-Mars energy encourages him to throw up his hands and not give a damn. This reaction can relate to his personal life as well as to his work. The fact that he is a Cancer Sun also energizes the transit, for Cancerians are more emotional than some of the other signs, so he may feel the emotional tension even more acutely.

Because the t-square takes place in his 4th, 8th and 11th houses, the home front, his partner's finances, his social life or friendships will be drawn into the focus of energy. This transit gives him an opportunity to become aware of the agony and confusion within himself. Once he *feels* the blocks he can begin to work his way out of them. He can rechannel the energy and use it to become more productive.

As soon as he gets through recovering from his Mutable planets, Mars will move into the Cardinal signs, setting off his natal Uranus, Mars, Moon, Sun and Neptune. The planets are not far from each other, and this transit will cause some inner agony every time it occurs. Because natal Uranus is at 5° of Cancer, the Mars transit will begin to affect it at 25° Virgo. This happens on July 2, 1980. His natal Uranus (Cancer) squares both the Moon (Aries) and Mars (Libra). This usually causes a person to become easily angered because the feelings are overly sensitive (Moon). Mars opposes the Moon in the natal chart and further emphasizes his anger. He is a Cancer, so he is already a moody type who responds to his environment with a great deal of sensitivity — feeling all that is going on around him and perhaps over-reacting to every-day life experience. During this kind of transit he may "pick up" the vibrations around him, making it difficult for him to diagnose whether the moodiness is in him or in fellow employees, or just in those he keeps company with.

Uranus also conjuncts his natal Mercury, the planet that symbolizes our five senses. Under a Mars transit, he may "go off" and respond too quickly; he may become exceedingly nervous; he may lose his temper easily and say things he may regret later. Because Mercury also squares Mars in the natal chart, he doesn't listen to others. He may jump to conclusions after only half-hearing what has been said to him. This can cause all kinds of hypersensitive reactions.

To add to the tension, Mars is quickly moving to square his Sun and Neptune. He may not know what he's doing (Neptune), and at the same time he's super energized (Sun). The tension may be unbearable for both him and his family.*

Once this energy is rechanneled, this cycle can be one of the most creative transit periods in the year. Because Mars hits both Mercury and Neptune at the same time, it could be a period of great creativity. This would be a good period for writing as this outlet would help him channel his energy so he can calm down. Once this energy is channeled, he will no longer have the energy to flare up at family and co-workers. He may be amazed at what he can accomplish.

As you compare your ephemeris with the list of Mars cycles, you'll notice that I've used a ten degree orb for all the Cardinal planets. As you

*If you are interested in reading more about natal interpretation of charts, see *Astrological Insights into Personality* published by Astro-Computing Service, 1980.

work with these cycles you may see that the more conscious and self-responsible you become, the earlier you'll feel the planets being activated by the transit. The period from 25° of a Mutable to 14° of a Cardinal sign will keep his Cardinal t-square alive. This entire period can be used creatively.

He has only one Fixed planet and that's Pluto. When Mars gets to 6° of a Fixed sign it will energize the natal Pluto aspects and they are all easy. This may indicate a period of sensitivity in regard to approval and respect (Leo). The hurt feelings will not easily become conscious because Pluto symbolizes our unconscious motivation. Because Pluto is nicely aspected, this may indicate a period when he wants to join his peers for some fun, or when he alters his goals to fit contemporary ideas of what a goal should be. He wants to be loved, because Venus sextiles Pluto and so does Mars and Neptune.

The Mars transits hit this chart several times a year. Because the natal planets are lumped together, this man will undergo a great deal of pressure during certain periods every year. When you see a client with a chart like this, you may see a certain amount of tension present in the body. As he learns to handle the tension, he can rid himself of it by allowing it to express on a more creative level. As he begins to work with his Mars energy, the physical tension may dissipate enough so he can begin to cope with the natal aspects and learn to use them more constructively.

These are not transits to be frightened of. He has felt this kind of tension several times a year ever since he was born, and will continue to feel it throughout his life. As you can see below, the transits repeat several times in 1980 and 1981. We all have a pattern.

High Energy (Mars conjunct, square or opposing natal Sun)
July 18 - Aug. 5, 1980
Nov. 28 - Dec. 11, 1980
March 23 - April 5, 1981
July 25 - Aug. 9, 1981
Super-Sensitive (Mars conjunct, square, opposing natal Moon)
July 8 - July 29, 1980
Nov. 20 - Dec. 6, 1980
March 15 - March 31, 1981
July 16 - Aug. 3, 1981
Talk-too-Much (Mars conjunct, square, opposing natal Mercury)
July 8 - July 29, 1980

Nov. 20 - Dec. 6, 1980
March 15 - March 31, 1981
July 16 - Aug. 3, 1981
In Love with Love (Mars conjunct, square, opposing natal Venus)
Nov. 23 - Dec. 22, 1979
Feb. 8 - March 8, 1980
May 8 - June 5, 1980
Oct. 14 - Oct. 28, 1980
Feb. 9 - Feb. 22, 1981
June 7 - June 24, 1981
Bad Buying Cycle (Mars conjunct, square, opposing natal Jupiter)
Feb. 20 - March 24, 1980
April 21 - May 27, 1980
Oct. 9 - Oct. 23, 1980
Feb. 4 - Feb. 17, 1981
June 1 - June 16, 1981
Problems with Authority/Men (Mars conjunct, square, opposing natal Saturn)
Dec. 1, 1979 - Jan. 8, 1980
Jan. 24 - Feb. 29, 1980
May 17 - June 11, 1980
Oct. 18 - Nov. 1, 1980
Feb. 12 - Feb. 25, 1981
June 11 - June 26, 1981
Super-Impulsive (Mars conjunct, square, opposing natal Uranus)
July 2 - July 21, 1980
Nov. 16 - Nov. 29, 1980
March 11 - March 24, 1981
July 11 - July 27, 1981
Loss of Perception/Meditation (Mars conjunct, square, opposing natal Neptune)
July 18 - Aug. 5, 1980
Nov. 28 - Dec. 11, 1980
March 23 - April 5, 1981
July 25 - Aug. 9, 1981
Unconscious Anger (Mars conjunct, square, opposing natal Pluto)
Sept. 8 - Sept. 23, 1980
Jan. 8 - Jan. 21, 1981
May 4 - May 18, 1981
Sept. 12 - Sept. 29, 1981

The main thing that can be learned from working with the Mars transits is that as long as we remain pushed and pulled by this transit we are not in command of our own personalities. Our personalities can be influenced by a perfectly predictable transit. We can be moved to anger and impulsive or petty action just because Mars is in orb of a planet symbolizing a part of our personality. The Mars energy needs to be handled consciously if we are ever to become self-responsible.

Jupiter Transits

Jupiter is a planet that symbolizes relating. It indicates how we open up, how we expand our consciousness. It indicates how we receive new information and material, how we react to the opportunities that are presented to us. The sextile and trine between Jupiter and a natal planet will often bring easy relating periods into focus. If we have easy natal aspects to any planet in the horoscope, we'll find opportunity when those aspects are energized by transiting Jupiter. If we don't the Jupiter transit will *not* indicate good luck!

• *Jupiter-Sun transits*

When Jupiter conjuncts our natal Sun, astrologers often say that something wonderful will happen. *That is not true.* When transiting Jupiter conjuncts the natal Sun it will energize any Sun aspect that you have in your chart. It will emphasize the qualities of your Sun sign and it will emphasize the activities symbolized by the house placement of the Sun. Jupiter always brings expansion—so it can indicate over-indulgence, a devil-may-care attitude, an overly optimistic attitude. It can bring opportunity in your life, but if the natal Sun carries hard aspects, you may not see the opportunity because Jupiter is energizing the hard aspects as well.

For example, one client of mine has Sun square Mars which conjuncts her Moon. When Jupiter came along to activate her Sun, an astrologer told her that she would be feeling wonderful, that this was a wonderful opportunity period for her, that she could expand her horizons during that period. However, my client felt extremely suicidal at the time. The Sun was active, but she wasn't feeling good enough about herself to relate to it because she was also coping with a natal Sun-Moon square as well as a Mars-Sun square, and she was feeling pretty self-destructive. Because she didn't know she was going to feel unhappy or depressed, she was really thrown by the transit for she was looking forward to this wonderful period the astrologer had predicted. She was not forewarned of the possibility of having to work through a natal aspect with a certain amount of intensity to it.

If the natal Sun is nicely aspected at birth, the conjunction of Jupiter by transit will bring with it an opportunity to open up your consciousness, to accept new opportunities. It indicates an excellent period for asking favors, for obtaining assistance from those in authority, for enlarging your outlook on love or life in general. If the Sun is not well aspected at birth, this period can also be fruitful if you know what you have to do in order to manage it. If you know a natal hard aspect is being set off, if you know what the aspect will feel like when it is re-emphasized, you can sidestep the hard issues and still look for the opportunity. This doesn't mean that you have to suppress your feelings, but that you put them into a different perspective.

For instance, should you have a natal Sun-Mars square and Jupiter is coming along to conjunct the Sun and square Mars, you know in advance that you may be prone to act (Mars) against your own best interests (Sun) during this period. As depression, or anger, or urges to respond to unhealthy activities manifest, you can examine why you need to do this, why you wish to remain unsuccessful, why you wish to "hurt" yourself. As this aspect is worked through, it will allow time to be spent in the pursuit of some more promising activity. Eventually, with a bit of practice, the transiting Jupiter will be used more and more productively.

The square and opposition of transiting Jupiter to the Sun manifest in a similar fashion to that of the conjunction. The square may bring with it more frustration or more excessive behavior. The opposition may color your activities with a feeling of loss. People push decisions, especially "choices," during these periods, and it is recommended that they hold off on decisions involving choice until the transit passes. The hard aspects can be turned into opportunities as well as the easy aspects can, but first you must sidestep the "hot potato" issues having to do with an "I don't care" attitude or a need for excess. Each transit of Jupiter to a natal planet will be colored by the natal aspects to that planet as well as the house placement of the planet. Each transit of

Jupiter brings openness, expansiveness, a chance to open up to new thought, new experience, new insights into your relationship needs.

• Jupiter–Moon Transits

Because Jupiter indicates an opening up, or an overrelating, or a devil-may-care attitude, when it transits in conjunction to your natal Moon, it tends to cause you to over-respond emotionally. The conjunction, square and opposition will make you painfully aware of any emotional difficulties you may have. It will bring those difficulties to the surface, enabling your conscious mind to feel the aspect. This consciousness helps us to understand attitudes we formed early in our childhood, so we can let go of the more unpleasant or unproductive ones.

If the Moon is nicely aspected, this transit signifies a rewarding emotional period. This person will be more than usually open to relate—it is therefore a good period to begin emotional relationships. If the Moon is afflicted at birth, this is a time to do some repair work.

When Jupiter transited my natal Moon (which is afflicted) I became painfully aware that it was difficult to reach out to others, to relate to the needs of others, and even to relate consciously to my own emotional needs. If we are ever to share ourselves with another, we have to understand ourselves. If we don't know what we need, how can we really be understanding of another? During this kind of transit, each of us can review our childhood relating experience. How did the family respond when you reached out in response to some emotional situation? If a child is cut off, or shut off, won't he grow to be shut off as an adult? And if that is the case, when will we let the old patterns go? This is a time for doing so.

• Jupiter–Mercury Transits

This transit is not too rough. It indicates an overly impulsive speech or thought pattern that will last for a period of weeks. If natal Mercury is unafflicted, this period would indicate opportunity through the communication channels—perhaps writing, or talking with important people, etc. The opportunity may be better interpreted after considering what kind of work the client does.

If natal Mercury is afflicted, there is a greater chance of misusing words, or misunderstanding words, or impulsively talking to the wrong people. Communication problems would be over-emphasized, so fears or lacks regarding the communication ability could be analyzed at this time.

In the case of an afflicted Mercury, the Jupiter transit will activate the natal configuration. Added to the natal aspect will be a touch of "I don't care" or a lack of interest in relating, a lack of concern for how your words may be taken, etc. The house placement involved with Mercury and the afflicting planet will be emphasized as well. We can move through this transit carefully!

• Jupiter–Venus Transits

When Jupiter conjuncts natal Venus, a tendency to fall in love with love occurs. We are now very open to new emotional experience. When the square and opposition take place by transit, we may become super sensitive about relating to a loved one, we may be tempted to cut off a budding relationship or we may try to push it to some kind of premature ultimatum. The aspects to natal Venus should be considered when reading the transit, for the transit will activate those aspects as well. If at all possible, we should try not to push situations that are apt to turn out poorly.

For example, if a woman has Venus square Uranus in the natal chart, transiting Jupiter may inspire her to end a relationship because she has a natural proclivity for that. If she has a relationship at the moment, and it is at all important to her, she can be forewarned about pushing too hard. The Jupiter influence may encourage her to relate excessively. She may not care enough about the relationship and may push for immediate satisfaction in regard to some ultimately minor issue. Being warned of the approaching transit, she can consciously decide whether or not she wants to take a chance on pushing the relationship or blowing minor situations out of proportion.

• Jupiter–Mars transits

This energy tends to cause an over-expansion of the Mars energy, inspiring a devil-may-care attitude regarding the action one takes or the sexual relationships that one pursues. This period may indicate an outrageous buying spree, or a giving up of a diet, or a binge on sugar, alcohol or drugs. Mars indicates the "I act" principle and Jupiter brings in the exhuberant energy that influences foolhardy activity.

The transit will spark any natal aspect to Mars, so this time period may become complicated. This transit can be used constructively to expand the action arena, to make expansive moves (within reason) on the job. It can be used to more fully enjoy sexuality and hopefully your partner is someone you can eventually "take home to mother!"

The transit may help you self diagnose any affliction to natal Mars because it can make us aware of a natal aspect. Jupiter invites us to *feel*, to relate to our natal aspects. Should someone have a natal Mars-Venus square, this would be a time to begin to relate to how the aspect pushes us to react to those we love. Once we can really relate to that inner fear or struggle, we can begin to cure it.

• *Jupiter-Saturn Transits*

This is a marvelous transit, for we have an opportunity to release some of our fears and cautions as a result of the contact. Saturn represents what we regard with caution, what we are afraid of, what influence the father had on our developing psyche during our first three years. It indicates our image of authority figures and how we relate to them. When Jupiter transits Saturn by conjunction, square or opposition, we have a chance to get in touch with those fears and cautions.

For example, if you have Saturn in Virgo, you may have some natural apprehension about your intellectual ability; you may not think you're good enough; you may not think you are capable of analyzing details; you may have developed a critical attitude regarding men in general. If the "male criticism" is apropos, a woman might have trouble expressing herself fully in a love relationship with a man. A man with the aspect would probably have difficulty expressing himself honestly with his male friends or fellow workers. In either case, the problem can be pinpointed during this transit. It may not be totally solved, but the transit can bring a part of it into consciousness. Little by little, the influence can be understood and used for some productive endeavor. Saturn becomes our friend and teacher, but we first have to notice the Saturn placement and give it some conscious attention.

During these periods, it is not uncommon to have some difficulty with finances. Often this is a good time to accept any additional responsibilities on the job even though the pay increase doesn't look as if it's coming. Eventually it will; eventually you'll be paid for the work load you are carrying. The company you work for now might not pay, but another company will pay for your working experience as soon as the transit breaks.

● *Jupiter–Uranus transits*

When Jupiter conjuncts, squares or opposes natal Uranus, the transit brings many possibilities of expression. Uranus symbolizes the part of our personality that is the most eccentric, willful or stubborn. If natal Uranus is nicely aspected, some change in behavior will be forthcoming and this change can be used in some constructive manner. If Uranus is afflicted at birth, the transit will emphasize the problems connected to the natal aspect. Since Jupiter indicates expansiveness, the transit would suggest a propensity for taking risks, for over-behaving, for being overly eccentric, or overly willful. How might that energy hurt the rest of the chart? What will it keep you from doing for yourself?

For instance, if Uranus squares the Sun in a natal chart, would this transit inspire you to become such an eccentric that you quit your job? Would it energize a need to take excessive risks—like hitch-hiking to the beach in order to save bus fare? Under this transit would you stop to consider that when you get in a car with a stranger, you might get more than just a ride? Here is our chance to change the outcome of our lives—because we have a chance to pick our times.

● *Jupiter–Neptune transits*

The natal Neptune position and sign tells us something of how we dream—what we dream of being, what we dream of doing, what our blind spots are, how our delusions, fantasies and creative ideas affect our lives. When Jupiter comes along by transit, the hard aspects (conjunction, square or opposition) will be the most influential to our growth. Jupiter brings expansion, and a devil-may-care attitude. Our relating ability will color our dreams. We may not perceive reality as those around us do—we may indulge in fantasies; we may pursue some ideal that is hopeless or impossible; we may fall in love with love; we may be blind in regard to what we need to be doing.

For example, a client has a Moon-Neptune square in her natal chart. Whenever Jupiter activates this square by transit, she falls in love. She reaches out to men who have no real interest in her. She opens up emotionally, and when the transit goes off, she falls to Earth with a big plop. As she learns to work with this energy, she will become apprehensive about starting relationships during one of her "prone" periods, for experience has taught her that these periods are unfulfilling. She can then meet someone she can "see" better, especially when the Moon-Neptune is free. The only transit that would make sense in her relationships would be that of Saturn, and that transit will bring a different set of problems with it. If we can't overcome a major transit, as Jung once said, we can live through it.

All things being equal, when Jupiter transits Neptune, it can be a period of opening up if the natal chart indicates the possibility. This would be expansion as it relates to meditation, creative looking within. It should be especially enhanced if Neptune is in an easy aspect to the Moon or Mercury.

• *Jupiter–Pluto transits*

Jupiter transits always bring an excessive or a devil-may-care attitude about them. The hard aspects are more active than the softer ones. Pluto is a common planet and sign to a whole generation, so the transit will not be particularly personal unless Pluto is involved in some other natal aspect. If Pluto is in sextile or trine to another planet, this period would be good for contacting masses of people, becoming involved in large scale communicative efforts.

If Pluto is involved in a hard aspect natally, then the Jupiter transit activates that natal aspect. It indicates that this person may be prone to responding to life stimulii from an overly-sensitive point and may not even be conscious of what he is reacting to. He may not be aware that he is over-reacting. The clue is that the Pluto position indicates what may be held in the unconscious mind that can spark off contemporary reactions. In order to remove the over-reaction to contemporary stimuli, the early childhood memories need to be acknowledged.

Pluto in Virgo indicates an unconscious reaction that relates to a feeling of insecurity regarding one's intellectual ability, or an unconscious reaction to criticism. What happens if this person hears a chance word in the office during a transit of Jupiter—will he tend to over-react? Has he taken stock of his ability lately? Has he evaluated his position as far as career is concerned? Does he have a good self image? If not it's time to take stock of it.

If Pluto were also in hard aspect to his natal Moon, would he be overly sensitive to what women might say to him or about him? Would he feel the need to control his emotional reactions, or even his emotional relationships? Pluto square the Moon in a natal chart often indicates the child of a controlling and manipulative mother. A male would have a certain inborn fear of losing his freedom to a woman in a relationship, and this feeling may result in attempting to maintain a relationship that includes manipulation of his partner. The control needs may not be conscious but he may feel defensive—as if he has to constantly insure his place in the relationship.

When the Jupiter transit comes along, this feeling would be intensified. It might be so intense that he looks for insubordination where there is none—or he looks for an offensive that hasn't taken place. Knowing the potential for these feelings, this is an excellent transit to use for working through at least a part of the problem.

Every time the transit reappears, it can be used to further free us of any energy block that may be standing between us and the fulfillment of good adult relationships.

• *Jupiter transiting the Angles*

The strongest angles in the natal chart are those formed by the first, fourth, seventh and tenth houses. Jupiter brings opportunity to expand when it hits the angles. Using a ten degree applying orb, we can begin to diagnose our times of opportunity and read the opportunity based on the signs involved and the houses that are affected.

First House. When Jupiter goes over the Ascendant, it brings an opportunity to expand the qualities of life symbolized by the Ascendant sign. The Ascendant (or first house) in the natal chart indicates how we begin things, how we appear to others, how we put our best foot forward. The conjunction will intensify these activities, and intensify the qualities of the sign ruling the first house. If the Ascendant is involved in hard aspects to planets in the natal chart, then the squares and oppositions indicated there will be activated, too. If the Ascendant is clean (or nicely aspected) this can be a marvelous period for developing career interests, relationship interests or both.

If the Ascendant is afflicted, career and relationship interests can be developed, but along with the opportunity for expansion is a need to "clean up" your attitude regarding the natal aspect. For example, if Mars squares your Ascendant, and Jupiter comes along to conjunct it by transit, you will experience the opportunity signified by the Jupiter conjunction as well as the activation of Mars square the Ascendant and transiting Jupiter squaring natal Mars. In keyword language, Mars square the Ascendant indicates that you act (Mars) against (the square) your new starts or new beginnings (Ascendant). So when opportunity knocks, you are apt to kick the gift horse in the mouth! Knowing your predilection for this kind of behavior, you can train yourself to restrain that kind of reaction, at least until after the Jupiter transit has gone! Because Jupiter will be squaring your natal Mars at the same time it goes over the Ascendant, you will tend to have an "I don't care" attitude, and probably won't react well to various business or career opportunities that may be presented. You might be so angry and out of sorts that you turn away any opportunity that knocks on your door.

These transits are important for when you look at your natal chart and see how your Ascendant is aspected (as well as your natal Mars position), you may notice that everytime you should be planning to make constructive moves, you are so upset emotionally that you don't use your energy constructively. You can train yourself to get past these sensitive periods, and in several years you'll begin to see the difference in your life experience. Even though you may not immediately solve your emotional problems, you can begin to make exciting moves on a career level, and those moves will begin to influence your development of a concept of self worth. As your feelings of self worth develop, as you begin to feel confident about decisions made regarding career, you'll also begin to feel a sureness of self that you may not have felt previously. So it's worth training yourself to use the Jupiter and Mars transits in some productive manner.

When Jupiter squares or opposes the Ascendant, another energy begins to manifest. On the square we usually feel a sense of frustration. Everytime we start something new, we run into blocks and brick walls. Usually when the Jupiter energy is activating the Ascendant sign, we have a tendency to project the worst qualities of the sign. People may react negatively because we are approaching them with a negative attitude. Whatever the Ascendant sign is, it's lower qualities are right out front.

If you have Leo rising and Jupiter squares the Ascendant from either Taurus or Scorpio by transit, the pompous qualities of Leo, the need for approval and all the behavior that manifests when we sorely need approval will be out there for the whole world to see. And, generally, the world won't accept our childishness. When Scorpio is rising, this is the time when the Scorpio Ascendant tells others what to do and how to do it. Scorpio has a tendency to come up looking righteous; it tells others how to live and how to behave. During the Jupiter square this person may offend everyone in sight. Sagittarius rising will over-emphasize the "know-it-all" attitude during a Jupiter transit. The Sagittarius Ascendant will try to philosophize to the 'nth degree. When questioned by others, the reply may be "God said it."

We can learn a great deal from Jupiter transits. When it sextiles or trines the Ascendant, we are usually in a good period, especially if the Ascendant is nicely aspected at birth. This energy can be put to good use if we understand what we are looking for. This would be a good time to further a career, to further personal relationships, if we have some idea of the goals we seek. Most people don't need counselling regarding the good aspects and transits, for they automatically use them well.

Fourth House. When Jupiter transits the fourth house, it simply enlivens the home front. This may indicate a desire to change homes, to redecorate the home, to change how one uses the home. If you are contemplating a new decor, it might be wise to wait for Jupiter if it's in the vicinity, because you may change everything again.

This Jupiter transit can indicate a change in how one views the scope of the home environment. For example, if you come from a family unfamiliar with socializing or coping with guests, you may find this a good period to start to learn how to do it.

Seventh House. The Jupiter transit to the seventh house will activate relationships concerning partners—both business and marital.

This may signify an interest in marriage if that kind of a relationship is on the scene. It may also indicate that you have more interest in relating to a partner, that you want to share more with your partner or that the partnership may be in the process of expanding, or making some constructive changes.

Tenth House. When Jupiter enters a ten degree orb to the tenth house cusp, matters of career become more important. This can indicate a promotion or an honor of some kind that is associated with your job.

This might be a good period to look for a new job, for the world has a favorable attitude. It's a good time to be expansive, open to new ideas, new approaches, new possibilities regarding what you can learn from an authority figure. This would not be a good time to plan a vacation, because it's important to be around when you are needed. Jupiter can only bring you what you have earned. If your job has been going well, it brings the potential for more honor than you can expect if you haven't been pulling your own weight.

Saturn Transits

The transits of Saturn can be the most productive of them all! Saturn is the great teacher and tester, testing our skills, our values, our philosophy, our very being. If we understand the reason for the testing—it happens so we can become conscious—the transit is a remarkable one. As we are tested, ideas are crystallized; we slowly mature; we slowly become aware of who we are, what we can be; we develop a sureness of self, a strong sense of character, a foundation of personality that can be depended upon throughout the most severe crises imaginable.

Saturn indicates the part of ourselves that we approach with caution. If you use a ten degree applying orb to define the transit period, you can spend a year evaluating some portion of your personality. Saturn retrogrades and goes direct, ending up on one of your planets for a least a year. If it is a major transit, or one that is particularly painful, I've noticed that Saturn retrogrades over that point several times to really rub in the experience! The first pass over the natal planet gives you a chance to get it together. The second and third pass give you time to clean up what has to be cleaned up in that area of your personality. If you didn't work on yourself at all, if you refused to mature, if you refused to take responsibility for youself in that area, the second and third pass will often cause some real pain. That pain could be the kind that occurs when you get fired from a job you like, or when you lose something you love.

When President Nixon lived through Watergate he had Saturn opposing his Sun. He didn't have to develop into a paranoid that kept files and tapes on other people so he could use information against them—but he chose to protect himself that way. His immature need for "protection" cost him his office. Many Capricorn people had Saturn opposing their Sun during that same time period and our productive Capricorns weren't punished; they didn't lose jobs and loved ones. They found this period to be one of serious evaluation.

We each have choices—we can go to the school of life and learn— or we can play hookey. We can do our homework or not—the universe doesn't care. Saturn has been called the Cosmic Cop and when the local men in blue don't get you, Saturn will—although Saturn may not get you in the manner you expect.

Saturn's biggest gift is probably that of personal crystallization. As we experience Saturn transits we can begin to know what we know. That is a personal truth, and it varies for each of us. In order to become self-centered or self confident we must know what we know. It is a gut reaction, a private internal process that can only be shared with someone who has reached a similar plateau.

• Saturn-Sun Transits

This transit will be in effect for about a year. During this time, you have the opportunity to take stock of yourself—who you are, what you are, why you are. The conjunction is especially important in regard to career. In the natal chart, the Sun indicates the "I am" principle and should be re-evaluated during this period. We should take a good look at where we are going, who we are doing it with, if we are getting what we need from life, if our career is fulfilling. If there are hard aspects to the Sun natally, the Saturn transit will be further complicated by those aspects.

The square acts a little differently, for it tends to activate difficulties associated with the Sun's *sign*. If you haven't gotten it together, if you are still immersed in the immature or unproductive qualities connected to your Sun sign, these qualities will manifest on such an obnoxious level that the people you know will stop you from continuing your pattern. Saturn square your Sun by transit gives you the option to excercise choice—you may become bitter and negative toward those around you because no one will buy your spoiled behavior, or you can use the experience to diagnose what you need to learn in order to further your growth.

For example, an Aries Sun might be too thoughtless, too

inconsiderate of others; a Taurus Sun might be too self-centered, too mushy, too clinging to the one he loves; a Gemini may be too experimental, new relationships may be so intriguing that the family is ignored and the family rebels; the Cancer Sun may over-play the little boy/girl act and get fired from a good job; the Leo may be too rigid, too pompous, too stuffy; the Virgo may be too critical, too analytical, etc. The rest of the world won't buy your act. Partners will leave you, employers will tell you to get it together or find another job. That's a part of Saturn.

You can be bitter and resentful and depressed during the entire transit and eventually it will pass. Or you can look at the "brick walls" you run into and consider them from a different point. (The brick wall usually manifests when our approach is wrong.) In this way, we can maintain our goals and make the necessary changes that facilitate our growth. Saturn hits the Sun every seven years and Saturn valiantly tries to move us out of our ruts. We change because we need to. The old adage, "necessity is the mother of invention," can apply here, for Saturn indicates the necessity for change.

The opposition brings a feeling of loss with it. If you have not been taking care of business, if you have not been working to further yourself from an honest point of view, if you have dumped on others to get ahead, if you have been shirking responsibilities, Saturn will cause you to pay some dues. If you have been acting in a somewhat mature manner, you may find yourself rethinking your position, and making plans to alter career or business decisions in order to expand your horizons.

In the process of self evaluation, the Saturn-Sun transits can be worthwhile watching. As you experience the conjunction, square or opposition of Saturn to your Sun, you'll begin to understand how you react to universal law. If you can make changes without resentment, and if you find you are not unseated during a Saturn transit, you must be okay. Saturn doesn't hurt if we learn how to change, if we are involved in the process of maturing. Those people who work well with a Saturn transit are self-responsible types who are not blaming the universe for their ills.

When Saturn aspects the Sun by transit, it indicates a period of self-evaluation. During this period you may become conscious of who you are and what you have to offer. This period often marks a serious turning point as far as career is concerned. People go into business for themselves; they may obtain new jobs that offer more responsibility.

The transit inspires a new concept of self worth. Marriages may be formed on this transit as well as new business ventures. Any obviously constructive decision will be a good one to follow.

I've heard clients say that some astrologers advised doing nothing important during a Saturn transit because it was not a good period for starting new ventures. However, I have found Saturn transits to the Sun to be one of the times when we take ourselves seriously enough to have the courage and stamina to do something we really believe in.

When the natal Sun is afflicted, the hard aspect will have to be considered at the same time that the Sun-Saturn transit is being worked through. This setup involves a double whammy experience, for we must work through a portion of the difficult aspect, become conscious of our energy pattern and rechannel it so that our energy becomes productive. Every seven years we experience a Saturn-Sun hard transit. Every seven years we have a chance to evaluate ourselves, to reassess where we stand. It can be an exciting proposition.

• *Saturn-Moon Transits*

When Saturn aspects the Moon by transit, it is a chiefly depressing experience! The Moon in the natal chart indicates how you respond to life, how you respond emotionally, what your emotional needs are. Those needs can be read according to the sign of the Moon, and the special emphasis of how we react to our emotional needs can be determined by the house placement and the other aspects to the natal Moon. The Moon symbolizes how your mother carried herself when you were a small child, and it symbolizes some of your ideas about women in general.

Saturn is the teacher, the tester, the Cosmic Cop and its transit indicates it's time for you to mature emotionally. In the natural zodiac the Moon rules Cancer and the fourth house. Saturn rules Capricorn and the tenth house. The fourth house always opposes the tenth causing some compromise to take place. If we view Cancer as the sign of Mother Nature and Capricorn as the sign of Father Nature, then the opposition between the two houses symbolizes a compromise between the two. It could be interpreted as the need to develop mature emotional responses. Saturn will crimp your style if you want to run off and wallow in immature emotionalism or in emotional reactions that don't relate to universal law.

All the great philosophies discuss Universal Law, and how we humans should learn to understand it. Saturn has something to do with Mother and Father Nature, and in astrological symbolism, Saturn represents our learning to understand universal law in our lifetime. Even though we put up a valiant fight to remain ignorant or to control Mother Nature and try to force her to play a subservient role to our will, universal law remains. Little do we realize that although we may appear to be winning—the Moon, our physical body, doesn't win at all when we go against the rules for too long.

We develop heart conditions and all those diseases that affect our innards. We become weakened and die, yet Mother Nature lives on. The trees grow and the birds sing in spite of all our pollution and attempts to poison the land that feeds and nourishes us. Father Nature, or Saturn, sometimes known as the "grim reaper", cuts us down.

When Saturn transits the natal Moon, we learn about our emotions. If we are not sophisticated enough to be learning about Mother Nature and universal law, we will be definitely learning about ourselves. During the conjunction, square or opposition, we may suddenly become aware of our bodies. Some feel the urge to lose those ugly pounds, to change the diet to something healthy; some decide to stop smoking or to get more sleep at night. Some find they don't have the physical energy to burn the candle at both ends anymore, for they can't make it on three hours of sleep, or they can't maintain the work load any longer. Saturn is saying slow down—live longer.

Since the Moon indicates the emotional nature, this time indicates a need to crystallize and consciously re-evaluate what the emotional nature *is*. This is the time to determine what your needs are, and whether or not they are being fulfilled. Chances are they are not. Your need for affection is a main consideration—not sex love, but *affection,* emotional caring, the arm around the shoulder, the understanding of your own personal crises, your emotional reactions.

If you are living with someone, you may feel pretty dour—for you may feel grossly unfulfilled. It's time to start talking. Although you may have little energy to put out to other people, you are looking for gobs of affection from everyone around you. This could be considered an "I feel sorry for myself," transit. Friends don't seem to help much either. When you need to talk, they're busy; or they don't seem to care about what you need. You may be tempted to end friendships, but before you do, consider that it's important to make new ones to add to those you already have during this transit. If we are to remain young, full of new ideas, full of spirit, we must bring new people into our lives for they help us grow; otherwise we get stuck in ruts, only seeing the same old crowd on Saturday night, and when those people get sick and die we are left alone and lonely. If we reach out at these times in our lives we can develop new insight as well as new friendships; the lifeblood grows stronger; the people we get to know are more versatile, and we don't sink into unnecessary death patterns.

We will evaluate our friends on this transit, however. We may drop a few of them because they no longer satisfy any of our requirements for friendship. We may discover that some old friends never really liked us. That sometimes happens. We will learn something about love on this transit and one of the major love lessons has to do with platonic love — the love you have for a relative or a good friend. It's not the same as emotional sex love, or the love we have for a child, but it is a valid form of love nonetheless. Because we need to learn something about this platonic love, some kind of a loss may take place during the year that Saturn transits the Moon. There are no guarantees as to what will happen, but here are a number of possibilities:

You may lose a female friend. This can happen many ways — she may move to another part of the country, and your closeness to each other becomes separated by expensive distance. You may lose a friend because she decides to drop you for no apparent reason; she may be so insensed that she won't explain the reason for the separation and you are left to sort out your feelings. Someone that you love as a friend may die suddenly, also leaving you to cope with the feeling of emotional loss. Older female relatives may die during this period as well — a mother, an aunt or a grandmother. There is no guarantee that your mother will die, dear reader — as she can only die once and this may not be her time. But if her health is frail, it may be wise to spend more time visiting her this year. Then in case she does pass over, you'll feel good because you were around. If she lives through your transit, she may need your emotional support, for somehow the Saturn-Moon transits indicate a time when your mother may be in a period of emotional depression that you can help her through. The same goes for the favorite aunt or grandmother.

The transit is meant to teach us something about love — how much it means to us, how much we need it, how important it is to share feelings with those we care for while they are alive. Much of the guilt we feel when we cope with the death of a loved one is the guilt caused because we didn't have time to be warm and caring until it was too late.

Many people are afraid to mention the word death—because we don't want to cope with it. However, death is a part of the living experience for death and life are forever interwoven. When counselling this transit, it is the responsibility of the counselor to ascertain how much the client is ready to hear. Many times clients overreact to the words of an astrologer, for the client endows the astrologer with supernatural powers. This transit doesn't guarantee a death in the family, but it does signify some sense of emotional loss.

Our emotional needs include a concept of emotional *satisfaction*. We can evaluate our "gopher" position and determine exactly how much we intend to "gopher" in the future when we undergo a Saturn transit to the Moon. This part of the transit is really wonderful, for we can eliminate a great deal of trash and tolerance of bad behavior when it is directed toward us. If we know people who treat us poorly, we tend to eliminate them from our life. If we are working in untenable conditions, we tend to discuss them more freely with employers. If business people treat us impolitely for no reason, they will hear about it during this transit!

One extremely shy client of mine surprised himself on a Saturn-Moon transit. Normally, he was shy and afraid of expressing himself around authority figures. He had a history of "taking low" and he was a reformed alcoholic. His pattern was to hit the bottle after he took a lot of crap on his job. He applied for a job that he really looked forward to doing and he was careful about his application because he wanted to settle in on a permanent basis. He was in his late forties and was aware that the job market gets more difficult as you get older. But he wasn't given the job he was hired to do. He had many talents and when his company learned that he was trained in another field as well they moved him into that position. So he marched up to the personel office and informed them that he would have to resign. He told me he wasn't angry inside, his stomach wasn't in knots as it was wont to be when confronting people in authority positions, but he didn't want the job they had given him. The supervisor was shocked, and because the company didn't want to lose him, they put him on the job he was hired for. He was elated! He called me to tell me this was a whole new experience for him.

The Saturn-Moon transit indicates that we learn something about taking our emotional needs seriously. We can cope with our needs without anger, without hostility, and speak with people as we never have before. Some women have reported that untenable love relationships have been ended during this transit—without malice, without rancor, just ended. This usually happens when an unfulfilling relationship has been going on for some number of years. This is not a transit where you jump down someones throat with no reason—this is a transit where you go "straight ahead" and deal with your needs because you know what they are. The lack of inner anger or frustration is a wonderful experience. The sense of emotional purpose can provide a whole new outlook for you.

If you don't understand the energy at play during the transit, this period can indicate depression, loneliness, misery, and sometimes a lack of energy that can even result in illness. You can ride out the transit maintaining those feelings, you can stay depressed, you don't *have* to learn anything about yourself, and eventually the transit will pass. But you lose the possibility of gaining real insight into your needs, into your self, into your self image. The transit is a beautiful one for it causes **crystallization and self discipline to take place. When you work with the** transit, you'll love it. Many clients and students have said they would like to have it back after they learned how to handle it. And it's true—it's a good learning experience.

The conjunction, square or opposition all work in a similar fashion. The conjunction is perhaps the most direct of the Saturn-Moon **experiences. The square brings with it some of the qualities caused by** the square aspect—those qualities of frustration and difficulty. The square seems to magnify some of our bad habits. It may intensify emotional reactions that are unhealthy or that need to be broken. People will have more trouble accepting you as you "cry in your milk" over the square. They may push you into becoming more conscious of your emotional concepts. Resentments will be a clue for us under this transit, as we become resentful when confronted with an energy that won't "gopher" our attitudes. Perhaps our attitudes need to be re-examined.

The opposition intensifies the aspect as it carries the qualities of the opposition with it. This quality is one of loss or temperence. Feelings of loss or deprivation may take place. Perhaps you'll get a harder "hit" from Saturn if you don't learn what you need to on this transit. This may indicate an emotional loss, perhaps a break in an emotional relationship. Perhaps you didn't take care of it when you had it. Saturn, as the Cosmic Cop, will make you "pay dues" if you deserve to. My feeling is that losses sustained under a Saturn-Moon opposition are losses that are necessary. Either you deserve the loss because you weren't emotionally mature enough to give when you should have, or you lose a situation that you no longer need—and because you can't leave, it ends without your permission. Time and self-analysis will bring the answer if you look for it.

• *Saturn-Mercury Transits*

As transiting Saturn begins to affect the natal Mercury position, the chief effect seems to be *coldness*. We begin to take our efforts at communication more seriously, and this emphasis seems to cause difficulties when we try to talk. Both external and internal influences are at play here. Authority figures, people whose respect and approval we seek, employers, employees, friends and lovers seem to require something different from us in the way of word communication. At the same time, the Saturnian influence stimulates an inner behavior that causes us to question our ability to communicate what we mean.

We may doubt our ability to communicate, or it may become so important to us that we pause over every word. Our friends may think we are cold and distant while we are searching for the word that would adequately describe the condition we mention. At any rate, we have to learn new phraseology, new vocabulary, new ways of expressing ourselves.

If we don't understand the energy that causes these sometimes dour changes to take place, we can spend a year offending people and turning them off! Because we are becoming more "serious" and because every word means something to us, and because we find communication difficult, the people we associate with may think we no longer wish to communicate with them. Words may come out harshly and sound bitter and cold. We may not mean to sound harsh, but others feel the venom or the coldness. If it's important to maintain friendships or relationships, we might pause a moment during this cycle to listen to the words we utter. Meanwhile, if we think we are being misunderstood in some way, if we are not heard the way we intended to be heard, we may cease any attempt to communicate, withdrawing into silence and assuming that no one wants to hear us anyway. That's just plain sour grapes!

This happens to be a difficult period for students of all ages. If you have a child in grammar or high school, he may not function at his best.

If you are in college or getting additional credits toward another degree, the work might be harder than you thought. This can dismay a seasoned student, for new study patterns have to be learned, concentration may be difficult, and past records of scholastic achievement may be changed. If you know you are to enter school under this transit, understand that this will be a more difficult period then most, and study accordingly. Work harder, be prepared to put in extra hours, and also know that the transit won't last forever. If you have to pass a difficult requirement, either allow it plenty of time or try to postpone the course until this transit breaks. Many a good student has flunked out of college at this point. It's unnecessary.

The transit can be used to establish new work patterns, new thought patterns, new ways of expression. It can be a year of serious conversations with those who count. At the end of this cycle, any constructive work done regarding your communicative abilities will pay off for you'll have new relationships, deeper understandings, and perhaps some new thought patterns.

On a more mundane level, when Saturn transits Mercury, some change in sensory perception may take place. Because Mercury rules the five senses, it is not unusual for people under this transit to complain of visual or hearing problems, or a loss of taste or smell. Each of us has to decide whether or not to accept a medical diagnosis during this period, or whether we think the problem will clear itself when Saturn removes the restriction. If a visual problem is diagnosed close to the end of the transit, it might be interesting to pursue the theory and see if the symptom disappears when the transit moves on. One of my students got glasses during the transit, and the prescription wasn't accurate at the end of the cycle.

The conjunction is the most serious transit for we take on new approaches more readily. Saturn, at this time, causes the development of a new approach to communication. Many of the new patterns we learn will be self inspired.

The square tends to bring growth because of friction. Authority figures, people who are important to us won't accept the poor choice of words, the immature expression of thought, the lack of clear thinking patterns.

The opposition tends to bring more loss with it for if you don't learn on this one, you'll lose something. The loss many have to do with prestige, or it may cause a feeling of being at a "loss for words!" New approaches to communication need to be looked into so development can take place. On a spiritual level, this period may inspire more silence—a need to communicate less verbally.

• *Saturn-Venus Transits*

Venus indicates what we want from life, our intellectual concept of what love is, how we appreciate being loved, how we appreciate beauty and art, what we like to surround ourselves with. When Saturn touches Venus by transit, values must be reassessed; our concept of love will be re-evaluated; we take a new look at what we want in life. Generally speaking, it's not a very happy period. If we use a ten degree applying orb, Saturn will be applying to a conjunction, square or an opposition to Venus for about a year. If you're lucky, you'll get several bouts with Saturn, for Saturn is kind enough to retrograde and give us several periods of Venus evaluation, especially if other aspects are natally involved with Venus.

The only way I can look at this period in life is with a sense of humor. Saturn aspecting Venus by transit hurts! We only become aware of our concept of love because it's missing! There are advantages to working constructively with the energy—for Saturn is a crystallizing energy, and we begin to develop a sureness of self as we begin to understand our basic needs in life. Since social activities are not going well (as Venus has something to do with our social life) this is an excellent period to forge ahead as far as career is concerned, for we are not enjoying anything else anyway!

Here's how it works. When Saturn gets within ten degrees of a conjunction, square or opposition to your natal Venus, you'll find yourself looking at husband, wife, lover, friends and family with different eyes. You'll begin to feel depressed because the chances are you're not getting your love needs satisfied. Isabel Hickey says of the natal aspect "that you have to learn how to give." As I began to work with the transit, her advice seemed to be the best around. When your own needs are not being satisfied, how can you give to others cheerfully? In the mundane sense, everything becomes difficult—if you see a blouse or a shirt in a store window, they don't have it in your size. The same happens with all needs, for purchases in general seem to be difficult and the most petty supplies are difficult to attain.

In the romantic sense, the body turns off. This transit has ended many basically good relationships especially when too much emphasis has been placed on sexual compatibility. The female turns off; she has little or no feeling in the vaginal tract, and even though she emotionally wants to make love, her body doesn't respond the way it did in the past. Those women who are brave enough to masturbate will discover that a normally sensual experience is not sensual at all!

The male has problems with erections or potency. He may feel a severe loss of sex drive. In this age of sexual emphasis, a year of this kind of response to sex can scare people. If the transit hits in the mid-twenties, panic sets in for most people worry that it signifies a future of sexual difficulty. When people live together during this transit, the partner living through the transit begins to wonder if he or she still loves the other; the partner who doesn't have the transit wonders if the Saturn-Venus person is seeing someone else, if the love has gone, if he or she is inadequate as a lover. If they don't talk to each other, the relationship can become quite tense. Once you understand that your body isn't functioning on this transit, you can go on to do something else. You can explain to your partner that this cycle will pass, that the relationship will come back to normal later. And if the love is sincere, the relationship will outlast any Saturn transit. This transit can be used for a reappraisal of emotional concepts. What is your definition of love? What do you want from a relationship? Is an orgasm the only way to indicate you love someone?

The transit will bring other changes as well. The decor of your home will change, the kind of clothing you like will change, or a new hair-do will come into being. You will view yourself differently. Your taste in music may change, as well as your taste in art and entertainment in general. You may want to move to another neighborhood, you may drop the friends who really don't satisfy your definition of friendship any longer.

The returns on new projects may not be as big as you might like them to be, but any career investment will pay off in the long run. Hard work and serious effort pays off later. The work will often be thankless—the compliments won't be coming in hot pursuit of a deal accomplished; friends may not be encouraging, nor may partners. We can learn the minimum that we need in order to survive during this transit. We may end up cleaning out the closets and ridding ourselves of all the unnecessary extras that become burdens over the years.

Social life can be a real drag—parties are boring, people seem shallow, we don't find the seriousness that we look for in others. This doesn't mean that you will be a social recluse forever, but that this period is wasted if you use it only on parties and social life. The only thing you want during this transit is whatever it takes to satisfy your new image, so you may be a bit testy or perhaps too hard on other people. Eventually you will soften and become more tolerant of others. This is an important formative period for you and you may take it so seriously that you don't have any fun.

This is a serious transit for women. If you need to begin to take care of your body, this is the time to do it. Venus can indicate upcoming problems with the feminine system—so a visit to the gynecologist is in order during a Saturn-Venus or a Saturn-Moon transit. Any problems that may crop up should be taken care of. This may be a period that sparks a new diet consciousness for we become aware of how we look.

When Saturn sextiles or trines natal Venus, we are in a somewhat serious period, but it is highly productive. This can indicate a period of harvest, for we can harvest what we have learned. We reap what we have planted on the more difficult cycles. Authority figures look upon our Venusian needs with approval, and we may attain some of our druthers.

• *Saturn-Mars Transits*

Mars indicates the action principle in the natal chart. The Mars position and sign indicates how we will attempt to express the needs of our Sun sign. The "I am" principle can only realize fruition via the Mars placement, for Mars symbolizes how we take action. "I take action to express myself," says Mars. We can think good thoughts and dream great dreams, all of which go unfulfilled if Mars doesn't learn how to express itself. When Saturn comes along by transit to conjunct, square or oppose natal Mars, we go into a year of crystallization—this transit teaches us to become aware of our action ability. Because Saturn is often felt as a restrictive influence, we find our actions stymied at this time. Authority figures seem to stand in the way or we may find our actions frustrated at every turn.

Because Mars also symbolizes our sexuality, we may find ourselves taking the sex act seriously. This may indicate a turning point in a younger person's life because "free love" or promiscuity is no longer acceptable. Someone who has had a very limited sexual experience may decide to change old attitudes during this transit. People who have accepted inadequate sex from a partner in the past may no longer be willing to do so. The transit lasts for a year, and as we look at the action principle, we can make changes. Saturn will restrict our action; it may cause an attempt to over-crystallize the qualities of the sign of our natal Mars.

For example, one of my clients is a Scorpio with Mars in Virgo. Natal Mars sextiles the Sun which is conjunct Jupiter. When the Saturn transit came to conjunct his natal Mars, he began to look at his profession more carefully, and decided he wanted to go into another business that would be more lucrative and perhaps more interesting. In order to get funding for his new business, he decided to approach his father. Even though there was a sextile between Mars and the Sun conjunct Jupiter, the Saturn pressure by transit was causing him to feel some apprehension about asking his father for money. He was afraid to approach him directly; he was afraid that his father would reject him. Saturn usually symbolizes authority figures and in this case the authority figure was the father. My client felt that dear old dad stood between him and the action he wanted to take. We discussed this attitude at great length, and he finally approached his dad, only to be completely surprised that his father was somewhat supportive. Scorpio people don't have fantastically enthusiastic parents but you'll never get anywhere if you don't try. A very practical Taurus once told me that if you don't ask, the answer would always be "no." If you ask you might get a "no" as well, but that puts you on the same level as you would be if you didn't ask. And if you get a "yes" you are way ahead of the game!

Sexuality becomes important during this transit because we need to evaluate what sex means to us at whatever stage of life we're in when the transit hits. Obviously, the transit will hit every seven years. Every seven years we must look at our actions and determine which way we wish to proceed. Young people tend to settle down after this transit has occurred. People begin to establish more constructive personal values after each Saturn cross over Mars. We are often pressured by contemporary social attitudes as they affect our sexuality. Young women want to be considered warmly sexual, young men want to be considered sexual super-stars, so both sexes tend to participate in sexual activity that is governed by social pressure rather than by personal needs. As we mature, as we change our views, we can become more individualistic, and we may begin to do those things that make us happy rather than trying to do something that interests our generation or that is only a contemporary fad.

The Saturn sextile or trine to Mars indicates a time when action taken will be supported by those in authority, by those who can help. This may be a time when we work diligently at our career.

• *Saturn–Jupiter Transits*

When Saturn conjuncts, squares or opposes Jupiter, changes take place regarding your concept of relationships. In the natal chart, Jupiter symbolizes how you relate, how you reach out to others, how you give of yourself when relating to loved ones, family or friends. Jupiter indicates how you will accept new information or new life experience. When Saturn comes along to transit natal Jupiter, a year will be devoted to the concept of relationships. It's time to mature in that department. It's time to crystallize, to become aware of how you relate. It may be difficult to receive new people at that time. It may be hard to relate to men in general. The aspects to Jupiter in the natal chart will be activated as well, so the transit can become more complex.

For example, if you have Jupiter square your Moon natally, the transit of Saturn will activate both Jupiter and the Moon as well as the natal square between them. Not only will you have to handle the Saturn-Moon transit, but you'll also need to develop an awareness of how you block or restrict your emotional responses in a relationship. You may now begin to realize that you don't relate to your personal emotional needs easily. This may be a period where your emotional needs are more suppressed or repressed than usual. The repression of legitimate emotional needs will eventually cause the development of a great deal of anger. This anger has to go somewhere—it may be expressed outwardly, or at worst, inwardly. When we repress our emotional needs, we don't allow ourselves a chance to reach out spontaneously. We put a great deal of pressure on the physical body. Eventually the body rebels and gets sick. This kind of transit may trigger an illness that has been waiting to manifest so you can get the message that you need to change. If that is the case, its wise to follow the signals your body gives you.

If Jupiter is not aspecting the personal planets in your natal chart, the transit of Saturn to Jupiter will merely indicate something about how you may limit your relationships. You may over-relate according to the qualities of the sign Jupiter appears in. For example, if Jupiter is in Virgo, that's a pretty critical and analytical sign. When Saturn transits Virgo, your relationships may become even more critical. You may over-analyze every experience; you may criticize everyone you know. Obviously, the people around you will rebel for no one likes to be analyzed or criticized all the time. You'll find that people respond better when you start using the more constructive qualities of the sign. Saturn's transit will help you become more aware of how this trait can be used productively. It's time to lift your consciousness a bit, to develop more mature traits and characteristics.

The Saturn Jupiter transit seems to have some effect on ready cash. Jupiter symbolizes how we reach out to receive and even though we reach out, the Saturn transit will limit what we get. It seems that we may not be paid enough during this transit, that we may be given additional responsibilities and no financial renumeration for our efforts. It sometimes happens that we don't receive our money on time, so this transit can be a serious one for those who are self-employed. Because the transit lasts for about a year, you may want to suggest that clients watch their budget more carefully, avoiding all unnecessary purchases until the transit is out. I've never heard of anyone being ripped off during this transit, for even though the money comes in slowly, it comes in eventually. And those who have worked for a low salary have been able to use the experience they gained to attain a better job and a much higher salary once the transit has passed.

• *Saturn-Saturn transits*

This is not really a transit per se. It's really a cycle, as all the planets have cycles relating to themselves. The planetary cycles will be discussed in a separate volume.

• *Saturn-Uranus transits*

In the natal chart, the Uranus placement indicates a behavior pattern. How you cope with your generation will depend on how Uranus is aspected to the personal planets in your chart. When Saturn comes along to conjunct, square or oppose the natal Uranus, you will get "called" on your behavior. If you have been behaving in a manner that doesn't complement your Mars, Sun, Moon or Ascendant, this may be a difficult period. The chickens come home to roost. This is a time to clean up your act. It's an easy transit to figure out—Uranus can be symbolized as your need for wilfullness, eccentricity or stubbornness. What are you being stubborn or willful or eccentric about? How might you be presenting yourself that may not be popular with authority figures, men, or the people in your life? How can you change? Saturn will activate and crystallize a change in behavior.

Obviously,this transit is more serious if your natal Uranus also aspects personal planets. If the Sun, Moon or Ascendant are involved, you'll be learning about the Uranus qualities of behavior at the same time you are investigating a Sun-Saturn transit, for example. The crystallization will certainly have something to do with maturity.

One client was almost killed on a Saturn conjunct Uranus transit. But before you misinterpret the statement, you must also consider that Uranus was in the first house in the natal chart and it also squared the Moon. The client was almost killed by a lover because no communication was taking place between them. He was so frustrated because of his own transits that he could no longer speak. Another astrologer warned her to leave town when the retrograde position would take place, as Saturn was due to retrograde back over the natal Uranus position and set off the aspect again. However, this person wanted to learn something and didn't want to leave town. As a matter of fact, the client couldn't understand why leaving town was necessary, because if predestination was a fact, then wherever she ran, the death transit would follow her. So instead of running, this client faced the situation, talked to her lover, apologized for some of her erratic and self-serving decisions that had been made in the past (the kind of decisions that people make when they have Uranus square the Moon by birth) and instead of being killed, she learned something about being an emotionally mature person. On a Saturn transit, you can learn to understand yourself and you can grow.

Other people undergoing a Saturn Uranus transit will not face death. Even someone with Uranus square the Moon at birth may not have an encounter that even closely resembles the one described above. That particular case involved first house natal planets. If the same natal planets had been in the second and sixth houses the transit may have taken place in a completely different area of life. The point is that Saturn can only discipline what warrants being disciplined. If behavior has been fair and open up until this point in time, if behavior has not been overly eccentric, then the transit can only encourage any growth that needs to take place. An astrologer is in a precarious position when interpreting transits from a fatalistic viewpoint. Astrologers should remember that we each have free-will, and with a client under an upcoming stressful transit, the astrologer has a chance to counsel someone about the potential constructive and not so constructive use of the energy at hand. The client is mature enough to make his own decisions as to how he wishes to use his energy. If we counsel in such a way as to leave the door open for the client's return, then clients will feel more comfortable about calling back when they need help or additional insight into the pressure of a contemporary transit.

• *Saturn-Neptune transits*

This is a rough transit to cope with. Neptune symbolizes what we dream of being. It symbolizes who we dream of being, our visions of a perfect career, of a perfect life, etc. It's main claim to fame is a certain nebulousness. It represents our world of fantasy, our fondest hopes and wishes. When Saturn comes along to conjunct, square or oppose Neptune, a crystallization of our dreams takes place. "Is that all there is?" is an apt description for what is taking place within. When this transit hits a young person, career goals and drives may be quite inhibited. If you are in college you may change your major, or self doubt may occur regarding your choice of careers. Disappointments may set in and the urge to forge ahead is drastically reduced.

When this transit hits in mid-life, you combine the normal average every-day mid-life crisis with a tremendous loss of hope. People who have worked in an industry for years finally get to the top and see what's there. The rose colored glasses are removed by Saturn, and reality strikes home. This reality usually brings disappointment. This person looks back and sees that all the previous years of struggle brought him to this juncture and it doesn't seem very exciting or fulfilling. Some people leave one career and go to another but it's really not necessary. Perspective is the key word here—we need to develop a new perspective. The vice-presidency is not the "valhalla" it seemed to be. And if it isn't, what is? What are your goals and expectations? What are your dreams? Isn't it time that they changed? Don't you know more now? Can't you develop a new outlook, or a new interest, or a new perspective?

When we get "there," wherever the "there" is, we always feel let down. When we first had our "dream" we were younger and we didn't know as much. Often we forget that we have grown to see life differently. The transit affects older people differently than those younger because the older person knows more. When we are in college, it is the kids in our college class that will take the world by storm. When Saturn hits Neptune in our forties and fifties, we're there and we see that the world hasn't changed as much as we thought it should have. This may be a time when the "older" person will begin to accept some of the spiritual philosophies because they usually see that the world doesn't change—Mother Nature and universal law are constant while people are disappointing.

Natal Neptune is nebulous—and we think that when we get "there" we won't feel pain anymore, or we won't be disappointed anymore, or our struggle will have been worth it. Saturn forces the nebulousness of Neptune to become crystallized. The vague dream we pursue suddenly has a name. And we still feel pain and disappointment.

The sextile or trine from Saturn to Neptune doesn't cause this kind of a reaction. Either aspect will reinforce other energies manifesting in the chart. These transits can be used to help crystallize (Saturn) the goals (Neptune) if the rest of the transits are supportive.

• Saturn-Pluto transits

Now it's time to learn about unconscious motivation. Pluto represents the unconscious motivation going on within each one of us. It also represents the value system for our generation. When we don't use our Pluto energy constructively, we tend to use it for control or manipulation games. If Pluto has hard aspects to the personal planets in the natal chart, those aspects will probably give a clue as to how we were taught to control our universe. Strong Pluto aspects may indicate a fear of life—this person is afraid that if he doesn't manipulate his environment, he won't know where he stands within it. The control needs are not necessarily "evil," but rather caused by a basic insecurity which comes out of our early childhood environment.

When Saturn comes along by transit to form a conjunction, square or opposition to natal Pluto, it's time to take responsibility for our motives, our control needs, our need to manipulate others. It's time to look within to discover some of our silly little games. It's time to crystallize that energy so it can be used constructively. It may be a time to let go. If letting go is difficult, a meditation course, or some exploration of metaphysics may help. Learning how to float or tread water may be of great symbolic value, for as we learn to float on the water we can begin to realize that we don't have to control the water, we have to learn to use it. Great inner re-evaluation may take place at this time. It's interesting to note that successful business people often change some aspect of their business under this one! They either branch out or transfer some responsibility to someone else. It's as though they know you can't survive doing everything yourself—the concept of sharing and cooperation comes alive.

This may be a period where tears are not uncommon. In your everyday life people do things that have some tie to your unconscious sore spot—some action is done and you find yourself in tears, or almost in tears. The incident can be used to spark memories that may lie buried, memories that need to surface so you can be free of them. Sore spots need to be soothed, not protected. They need to be looked at and named so they can be let go. The transit can help free us from long forgotten childhood memories that linger in the unconscious keeping us tied to a particular environment or attitude.

Pluto represents unconscious energy or drive, and the sextile and trine from Saturn can help us bring some of the energy into play from a more conscious perspective. Natural talents may be developed during the hard or easy transits, as Pluto symbolizes the creative urge within.

• _Saturn transiting the Angles_

As Saturn moves around the chart, a cyclic energy is brought into focus. Grant Lewi has discussed the transits of Saturn as they affect the angles in the chart. I feel that the Saturn transits to the first house are the most important. However, the Saturn transit to the angles requires that we listen to those voices both outside (from friends) and to those voices from within—and they whisper, "Change."

First House. The Ascendant symbolizes how we put our best foot forward—how we act when on our best behavior. It can indicate how we function as we work and how we appear to others. It also gives some indication as to how we are treated by others. The Ascendant symbolizes the persona or the "cover" that protects us as we go about the business of hiding the vulnerability of our Sun and Moon sign.

When Saturn passes over the Ascendant, it brings a crystallizing kind of energy that forces us to put our money where our mouth is, as they say. Using a ten degree applying orb you have about a year of Saturn coming to the exact conjunction to your Ascendant. During that year you may notice that you are stopped or restricted any time your "best foot forward" is immature. Saturn is a serious symbol and brings a note of seriousness to any new beginning. It indicates that you can now take what you say and do more seriously, and you may begin to do things that you really believe in.

If you have not been mature. Saturn will play the role of Cosmic Cop and set you back a pace or two. Especially when Saturn squares or opposes the Ascendant, you will get any comeuppance that you have been asking for. If you learn to listen to the Saturn message, you can divert any potential disasters because Saturn is the symbol of teacher as well as the symbol of the grim reaper. The universe is not sadistic, just realistic, and if you show some promise of listening to Mother and Father Nature, you will learn a great deal from a transit of Saturn to the Ascendant.

If you have been goofing off, or if you are holding on to the past, or if you have been irresponsible as far as career or personal life is concerned, Saturn will bring you a message. You may begin the transit by running into trouble, blocks, brick walls, uncooperative people. If you look at the problems you run into with the question, "What is the message I'm to learn now?" you can understand how it's necessary for you to change. If you don't learn, the brick walls get higher, the obstacles get bigger until you get stopped.

Saturn going over the Ascendant indicates a chance to rebuild yourself from the inside out. It brings a chance to take yourself seriously. It may signify a change in career, a change in your approach to life, a chance to redetermine ideas, goals and attitudes. This can be the start of a new interest, a new anything. This transit can indicate a very serious change in your lifestyle. Some people get married during Saturn's influence, some become parents, some become single. It can be an exciting period although it is one of serious changes rather than the more frivolous kind. Constructive decisions such as deciding to get married should not be avoided because you are taking yourself seriously. People who marry during this time are not taking vows lightly or marrying on the spur of the moment.

Fourth House. When Saturn transits the fourth house cusp, you have a chance to put the material you've learned in the last seven years (since Saturn crossed your Ascendant) into practice. The chances are you will be able to add this knowledge to your career interests. You may find you no longer like your environment, and you may be making plans to move. You also may decide to buy a home or you may decide to make some serious alterations in your home so you can use it more to your advantage. This may also be a time when you seriously want to evaluate the effect of your early childhood environment on your adult personality, and you may wish to begin therapy of some kind. This kind of evaluation is not sparked by a desire to blame parents for the kind of person you are, but to analyze the environment to understand what it is that you reach for, or what factors you bring with you that may keep you from having the fullest kind of life possible for your chart.

Seventh House. When Saturn comes into a ten degree orb of the seventh house cusp, the heart turns to marriage. Some people view their marriage or partnerships with an overly serious attitude. Some people want to become single again as this transit approaches. Some people want to get married as they begin to view the idea of a marriage partner with seriousness. This can sometimes indicate a client who wants to get married at all costs, who chases the potential partner and literally scares him away. Both men and women have done this—for male clients have proposed on the second date, and female clients have pursued men in a similar manner to a vulture looming over some poor unsuspecting guy. Marriage is being viewed seriously! That's okay as long as you understand what you are doing.

This is a time to view partnerships seriously. If you are in one, it might be a time to start talking about what you want from it. It might also be wise to listen to the other person involved. If we want to be heard, if we want equal time from someone we live with, we also must learn how to give it. If we don't want our serious moments to be made fun of, we have to stop making fun. The Saturn transit brings a new look at partnerships.

Some people marry on this transit, and that's okay providing they are not grabbing someone off the street with a butterfly net. Others resent marriage during this transit, because when Saturn transits your seventh house, it is usually opposing your Ascendant. It can cause one to feel that partnerships are limiting, or that one must give up a part of oneself, or one's desires to make new beginnings, in order to have a partnership.

Tenth House. When Saturn gets ten degrees away from the tenth house cusp, it is beginning to affect the public image or the career image. Some people reap honors under this transit. Some people develop a sense of purpose as far as career is concerned. Because Saturn is also the Cosmic Cop, those people who have not been able to deliver on the job may be let go under this transit. One client called me to say that she had been fired the day Saturn exactly conjuncted the tenth house cusp. Because she had begun to look at herself in perspective, and had begun to assume responsibility for her actions, she noticed that this was the one job she had where she didn't deserve to be fired. She told me that she should have been fired from the others—and that this firing was not justified. She figured that it was "karma" and that she was paying off some past debts. I don't know if I agree with that, but I listened to her story and counselled that she go right out and get another job. She did and she's been there ever since. I must mention that this is a client who had a record of being unable to stay at a job—she moved from one place to another, running anytime she felt that the fellow employees were becoming too inquisitive.

Saturn transiting the tenth says that you are beginning to take career goals seriously, and it affects us differently at different ages. For the young person, the transit can indicate a serious dedication to some career goal. For the older person, it may signify a change in career. When Saturn hits the tenth it brings the honor that we have striven for up until this time. A fifty year old man will react much differently than a twenty year old. However, the transit should not be read as disasterous, for it isn't. It can be symbolic of whatever we have put into our lives up to that point.

Uranus Transits

The transits of Uranus bring freedom and potential for a certain kind of rebirth. They symbolize stages of liberation and freedom. The energy of a Uranus transit helps us break the rigid patterns we have been programmed with. It sparks new ways of handling crisis and growth. This transit brings changes, and we will learn how to change or suffer the consequences! Nothing goes as planned; nothing seems stable. On the other hand, opportunity comes knocking and people offer us new ideas, new ventures, new ways of thinking. If ever we are to learn to bend, now is the time! If we don't bend, we might break.

Some people successfully remain stick-in-the-muds through this transit, but they miss out on all the growth potential. They miss the new people and the new attitudes. They miss out on new insights and different ways of handling old problems. You've all seen interesting older people who are a joy to be around, and you've all seen stodgy old people that all the relatives avoid—those folks who become senile and who are generally thought of as bores. Well, there's the difference between handling Uranus transits openly or stubbornly. You can hang on for two years—for Uranus will be in a ten degree applying orb to any natal planet for two years. You can remain stubborn during this period and never change. Or you can jump on the bandwagon and enjoy this transition.

• *Uranus–Sun transits*

This transit is both exciting and invigorating! You'll never know what's happening from one moment to the next. Your work day will probably be disorganized; your social life may be in chaos. But there's something to be learned here. When Uranus opposed my Sun, I found the transit difficult at the beginning. I would go to work in the morning and never accomplish what I had planned. Something always happened, some emergency always came up, and the same pile of work was on my desk in the afternoon that was there in the morning. I was getting pretty frustrated. I began to realize it was time for me to learn how to handle the challenge of change. I had been accustomed to planning my week as well as planning my workday. I didn't like interruptions or diversity. It was time, said Uranus, to learn how to handle such events. I felt that management positions needed managing and structure and previously I had bitten off more than I could chew as far as responsibility went. It was during this period that I learned to work with my superiors. We had rush jobs—and I learned how to deal with "hot rushes." I would share my responsibilities and work load with my department head, by letting him know about the pressure instead of trying to handle it all myself. Together we decided which "hot rush" to handle first.

In my personal life, plans were going awry all over the place. If I made plans to meet a friend for dinner, either I couldn't make it or the friend couldn't. I learned to develop Plan A, B, and C. Up until that time, when I made plans that were cancelled, I was crushed. I couldn't get motivated quickly enough to do something else with my time. I learned how.

I was also going to night school and tried to study after returning home from work. The plan was that after I studied for my class, it was time for dinner and taking care of the household chores. My next door neighbor, however, decided that 6 p.m. was the time for loud music and partying and I learned that studying philosophy to the beat of a conga drum wasn't easy. I got angry and, of course, could no longer concentrate on my studies. Then I learned to study when he was quiet and to do the dishes and the vacuuming when he was noisy. My schedule bent to any occasion. I began to think, "Well, I can't do this, but what *can* I do?" Suddenly my life changed. I became so bendable that sometimes I shocked myself. My schedules (as well as my house) haven't been the same since.

As soon as the bending began, new people came into my life— people who were interesting, people who opened new doors and new channels of communication. These people didn't stay in my life forever, but as they passed through they gave me something and I hope I gave them something in return. This transit can be exciting if you want to open new doors, if you want to investigate new avenues, if you want to explore something new.

Many clients have talked to me about this transit because they hurt. Bending is difficult and change is frequently viewed with apprehension. I've told them all about my experience with Uranus and how the transit to my Sun got me started in the process of coping with change. The feedback from them has been heartwarming for they began to view "change" differently too. This transit is especially difficult for people who too closely equate personal validity with their job status. As soon as the work load causes too much stress and change, these people begin to feel invalid. That's not what Uranus is about!

Not all stories about Uranus transits are successful though. One woman client was experiencing Uranus opposing her Sun by transit. Although it was time to change her life, and although she had been talking about it for years, she just kept talking and didn't do anything. She had been a part of an unfulfilling marriage and it was time to get out. She knew it, her friends knew it, her children knew it. She didn't—and became so severely ill she almost died. As she recovered from her illness she began to realize that she had missed the boat, that she had to remove herself from her difficult circumstances. We talked about her evaluation of the illness and she felt that she may have avoided it had she left when her inner self told her to go. She felt that her body had to rebel in order that she become aware of how serious was her need to be free.

Some astrologers may tell you that Uranus transits indicate sudden and quick events in your life. People do seem to react strangely under a Uranus transit, but since Uranus takes so many years to move through a sign, perhaps the erratic behavior we observe is only seemingly erratic. People who don't know us may be surprised when we finally get the energy or the courage to do something we've been thinking about for years. We change inwardly under this transit, and as our inner conviction grows, we pick ourselves up and move from New York to California or vice versa. We leave old marriages and try living alone or vice versa. Big changes are made. Usually the change is a constructive one for us although our actions may seem strange to others. We feel liberated; we feel free.

During this transit it's important to keep a perspective in mind. What are your goals? Do you understand that you are changing inwardly? Outer changes are only physical manifestations of inner change. A facelift won't improve a bad marriage or a bad self image.

Rigidity needs to go. On the other hand, its not wise to throw the baby out with the bathwater! In Voltaire's *Candide,* Dr. Pangloss says all change is for the better. But that is absurd. Change is only "better" when we know why we do what we do. The face lift won't make the forty year old lady any younger. Better that she consider her value as a mature woman.

• *Uranus–Moon transits*

Any rigidity in regard to our emotional responses comes to the fore during this two year transit. We learn new ways of expressing ourselves emotionally. We may be quite surprised about how differently we feel. We may not be able to control our emotional responses or reactions, much to our surprise or chagrin. Where we were once able to keep our "cool" we may find we have to control—and tears or anger or warm feelings may surprise us. We may jump into relationships too quickly or pressure ourselves unnecessarily about love. We may not handle our emotional lives as we once did. We may be overtly abrupt, harsh or too emotional. When Uranus conjuncts, squares or opposes the natal Moon, others may have difficulty relating to where we are coming from. We may act strangely toward people who think they know us well.

The strange love affair should be approached with caution for we don't know the outcome. Obviously this facet of the transit is more important in big cities than it is in the country for there we meet the "handsome stranger" more readily. It's advisable to check into the new love's background for it may not match his image. The person who comes into your life now may teach you something important, or may mean a great deal to you, but the relationship may not last forever. It may end as abruptly as it began.

The transit brings a great deal of physical tension with it. The body may react to spasms of any sort during this period—the muscle twitches, eye lids twitch or maybe your upper lip does. Your attention span may be shorter or you may be easily bored with people.

The key to growth here is learning how to expand your emotional horizons. Learning to accept your own spontaneity is better than being withdrawn and insecure because you feel apprehensive about the changes going on within. The emotional responses learned at your mother's knee can be let go in favor of a more open attitude. The change will be signified by the Moon's sign.

• *Uranus-Mercury transits*

The hard transits to Mercury from Uranus may spark many types of nervous disorders. Ticks or spasms can also affect the facial muscles, the eyelids, the upper lip. The hearing process or speech pattern may change. You may wind up with disorderly sentences. You may feel mentally hyper and feel some mental stress or tension because the mind is functioning too quickly, or differently than you are accustomed to. Some clients have worried about mental stability for we tend to over react to others. If this is a problem, the energy may need to be channeled in some creative area.

Clients who dislike the Uranus-Mercury transit find it a difficult aspect because of the changing concept of mental stability. If the natal Uranus doesn't aspect Mercury, the transit indicates a worry that may originate deep in the recesses of the mind concerning mental stability. Seldom is this fear shared with friends, co-workers or even doctors. Those who have activated a natal Mercury-Uranus aspect because of this transit have been concerned about their stability before and may have already sought help through therapy. People experiencing the energy for the first time may react more strongly than those who have the aspect natally.

Metaphysically speaking, any hard circumstance of life can be cured if the *cause* of the difficulty is faced consciously. I feel strongly that this transit indicates the presence of phenomenal mental energy and unless the energy is channeled, it will make the recipient feel unstable. Uranus energy is a freedom or a liberation energy and aspecting natal Mercury, it frees up and speeds up the communication process. The mind races forward like a car out of control on a highway. As soon as this energy is channeled, the energy is dissipated and can be used constructively. It doesn't much matter how we use it for as long as it gets used, something constructive will come out of the experience. Any hobby, any class you want to take, a writing or painting project — any creative endeavor sparked by career needs will help channel the energy. The boon for the work we do occurs when stability is restored.

Because the mind functions so quickly during this transit, we may not stop to listen to others and we may express ourselves unclearly. Misunderstandings on the job can take place unless we make a conscious attempt to listen carefully, or to ask people to repeat themselves before we jump to conclusions. The transit can also indicate the "blurting" disease and the symptoms are that we start talking about something foolish and can't stop! Once in this position, it may be wise to admit the blooper and change the subject if you can. Trying to clean up the mistake usually results in getting in even deeper.

The transit can free the mind of many preconceived notions that were developed in the early childhood environment. You may find yourself communicating differently when the transit is over. You may find that the natal aspects to Mercury are liberated in some way, or that this period indicates a time in your life that can be used for the freeing up of natal blocks. As the concepts from childhood are let go, you can begin to think and speak and hear the way you want to, using the energy symbolized by your natal Mercury sign.

• *Uranus-Venus Transits*

Venus represents the ability to appreciate being loved. It indicates how we want to be loved, what our intellectual or "heady" concept of love is, how we are able to give and share with our loved ones. When Uranus comes along to conjunct, square or oppose natal Venus, the love facet of our personality can be liberated or freed from previous ideas or structures. We may be too willing to jump into something new because we want to try out our new ideas, our new freedom, our new liberation.

Many people fall in love with a handsome stranger or lass on this one. Some leave home and family to pursue the dynamic ideas that have just been discovered. However, this transit indicates an inner freedom, a change in consciousness or attitude that is developing within. These qualities and changes may not necessarily be within the wonderful partner that you may chance to find. If this new love beckons you away from job or home or responsibilities and is real and meaningful, it can wait until the cycle is over. When the transit has passed, if you still find your love attractive, changes and compromises can be made in your life style. The love that occurs during this transit is often a feeling of the moment. It can be a valid and important experience, but it may not be a lasting one.

Women sometimes put themselves in compromising situations under a hard aspect of this transit. These women fall for the tall dark stranger and never check out his credentials, never explore the gentleman's background, and find themselves in a second rate position. One client married a man after a whirlwind courtship of about three days only to find herself in a brothel. The man she married was a pimp. It took her three months to get away from him, and several years of therapy to get over the blow to her emotional being.

Not all relationships formed under this aspect will be so dire; but I recommend that women do extra checking on the wonderful man they have just met. First, whirlwind courtships usually indicate the male is exerting unnecessary pressure. Does he want to meet your parents? Why not? Does he have a job? Have you called him? Did he give you an extension number? Why not call the switchboard operator and ask for him by name? He can use an assumed name if he is the only person answering an extension. Is the company he works for listed in the phone book? Does the operator answer the phone quoting the company name? Why not? Does he have a home phone? Do you have his number? Is the phone listed in the phone book? Does the address match the phone number?

Time tests all love. True love can stand the test. Con games can't. If the love isn't there, then the contemporary song applies, "If you're not with the one you love, love the one you're with." Women who fall prey to the whirlwind romance are in an inflationary period because the Uranus energy is sparking the Venus desire nature. Men who are swept off their feet by an alluring woman are feeling the same thing. A sense of pressure and excitement prevails.

This transit hits men and women at an age or a time in life when desperation seems its strongest—a woman who has never been married who wants to get away from home, a stranger in a new city, etc. The man who is unhappily married, or who feels cheated of life in some way, the man who didn't expect marriage to be what it turned out to be, or the man whose career has been unfulfilling may be a victim to the love he meets during this transit.

When a man falls in love under a Uranus-Venus transit, it usually happens with a wonderful, sensual and alluring kind of woman. She represents all the things in life that his wife doesn't. He may have an undeveloped anima image. He may be still chasing the maid in gossamer, not dealing with the reality of relating to someone on a seven day a week basis. He may be stuck in a job he doesn't like, and this is a new intrigue that excites him. His concept of love is changing and it's hard to convince him that it didn't change *because* of the new love. He probably met her as he was in the process of change, but he may project his changing consciousness onto her, giving her credit for it happening in the first place. This new love may carry more weight than is rightfully hers.

The woman who is susceptible may be coping with an undeveloped animus image. The Cinderella story, where the prince saves you from your fate is an exciting concept. Being swept off her feet, being told she is beautiful and exciting makes her feel great. It can be such an exhilarating experience that she is so busy feeling good, she never looks at the guy.

On a more serious note, during this transit our concept of loving is changing. We develop an idea of what love is when we are children and the concept is developed because of our relationship with our parents as well as their relationship with each other. Under this transit, that concept changes—either it matures or it changes. Any natal aspects to Venus will further enhance the transit and add to the story.

Not all astrologers agree with this idea, but I feel that Venus symbolizes a psychological effect of the mother on her child as the child develops an ability to love. If this child carries a strong unconstructive influence from the mother (which would be indicated by hard aspects to natal Venus) this transit can also symbolize the chance to be liberated from the patterns picked up from the mother.

• Uranus-Mars Transits

Mars symbolizes the action principle in the natal chart. It is also symbolic of our sexuality—what we need from sharing the sexual experience with another person, how we express ourselves in that department. When Uranus moves into a ten degree orb to hit Mars for two years, it has a liberating effect on both the action principle and the sex drive.

Action includes how you act on your job, how you act socially, how you act out any energy you project into the universe. When Uranus hits Mars, action can become a bit "hyper" and out of sync. It can bring us energy that can be used as the foundation for creative action if it is channeled properly. It can promote unchanneled behavior that could be termed phrenetic because you may jump into activities without thinking them through or approaching them with any perspective.

The transit can emphasize the sex drive and most people who are sexually active before the transit become even more active. A word of caution however—for sexuality can become so intensified during this period, emotional and sexual involvements may seem to be most inspiring when most of the inspiration is coming from you. You can bring some really intense energy into any sexual relationship you form, but the intensity won't last forever. When the transit moves off, your sex drive will fall back to a similar level to that before the transit, and the wonderful, fantastic partner you found may turn out to be just an average lover. If you fall in love during this transit, it may be wise to consider factors other than sex before commiting yourself to the relationship on a permanent basis. Marriage or expensive living together arrangements may be better left to the time when the transit has passed. If you share mutual interests in other departments of life, if you are sincerely in love with each other at the same time that the sexual fascination is taking place, you can develop a permanent relationship at this time. But if the relationship is only sexual, it may fall apart when the transit is over.

The liberating effect of Uranus hitting Mars involves the releasing of the sex drive, as well as a freeing of action patterns. Actions can become very creative. Energy can be used differently. We can rid ourselves of fears of sexuality, or of sexual apprehensions brought into our adult life because of early childhood mores or environmental conditioning.

The transit is made easier or more difficult and complicated because of the natal aspects to Mars. The natal aspects will also partake of the Uranus transit. The ability to consciously "feel" natal aspects can surface so that blocks to action can be worked through.

• *Uranus-Jupiter Transits*

Jupiter symbolizes our ability to relate, how we reach out to experience the environment around us, how we share our experiences with others, how we recognize opportunities in the world around us. When Uranus comes along to make a hard aspect to Jupiter, unusual opportunities may manifest. Relationships may change, the relating concepts may change, and more freedom to relate is available.

Uranus indicates a process of change and these changes are made in what may seem to be an unorthodox or unconventional manner. Other people may react to you strangely during this period, for you may not relate the way you did in the past. Uranus indicates your eccentricities, a certain wilfulness or stubbornness, and when this energy is applied to Jupiter, your relationships may become too abrupt or too eccentric. Reaching out to others may be abrupt or unplanned.

You may find yourself enlarging your circle of friends because you bring new people into your life in a way you never did before. This may be both good and bad! You may meet wonderful new people with whom you develop long term friendships, or you may open up to the wrong people or to people you have little in common with when you eventually get to know them.

The wonderful opportunity comes when you realize that you will eventually be more open and receptive to building new relationships. You will eventually be able to leave behind the concepts from early upbringing. Relationships can develop, not because Mom told you they could, or because it would be socially advisable, but because you personally feel the need for it.

Business opportunities may develop as well, but you won't find these opportunities occurring in a particularly orthodox manner. Perhaps many opportunities to develop your career will occur, forcing you to figure out how you can take advantage of them all. It may be a good idea to try to follow through on as many as posible because not all offers made to you will hold water.

If you have hard aspects to Jupiter natally, those aspects will also be activated by the transit. You will have a chance to become consciously aware of how you naturally handle your relationships. For example, if Jupiter squares the Moon natally, you may be accustomed to regarding your emotional needs and responses with difficulty, for it is normal for you to play down your immediate needs in favor of those of other people. During the Uranus transit, the Jupiter–Moon tendencies can come to the fore, and you may become acutely aware of how difficult it has been for you to learn how to relate. If that is true, you may even feel some anti-social feelings; you may over-react to people you don't care for, or to business situations that are difficult for you to cope with. These difficult responses can help you learn how much you may have suppressed in the past, for the same situations may have been tolerated before the transit. As you become more interested in developing sincere and genuinely open relationships, you'll begin to feel better.

• *Uranus-Saturn Transits*

This is a lovely transit for it combines maturity with freedom and liberation. Saturn symbolizes what we regard with caution and apprehension, the slow or small organ of the body, the fears and inadequacies we feel. Saturn can also symbolize the psychological effect of the father on the child's psyche.

Our parents have both a physical and a psychological effect on all of us as we grow up. Early in the life of every child, the father's apprehensions and fears, the father's attitude regarding authority figures and his image of self worth is transmitted to his child. As the father changes, he offers new images to his children, so brothers and sisters may each carry a different psychological impact from the father image.

During the transit of Uranus to Saturn, these fears and apprehensions can be cast to the winds or finally let go. This may be a process that takes many years, but each time that Uranus conjuncts, squares or opposes Saturn, another stride forward takes place and some new freedom occurs.

If Saturn also aspects the personal planets, such as the Sun, Moon, Mercury, Venus or even Mars, it becomes possible to break the strength of any natal hard aspect at this time as well.

As we all experience the Uranus-Saturn transit for two years, we have ample opportunity to make these changes slowly because they don't come and get us. The key words are liberation and freedom, for our fears will disappear. Aspects of life that caused apprehension in the past will no longer do so. The fear of disapproval from the authority we feared all these years will change and we can begin to calmly confront situations that caused misgivings in the past. The house and sign Saturn occupies will be helpful in understanding the needs of the personality that will emerge.

Because Saturn indicates the smallest or most frail organ of the body, we can diagnose our weaknesses by both the sign and house placement of Saturn. Preventive medicine may be used during this two year cycle to help avoid medical problems. Obviously, if we mishandled our bodies for years and years we may not be able to avoid some kind of medical treatment to compensate for the abuse. If our bodies are in fairly good shape, common prevention can help avoid further damage.

For example, those people born with Saturn in Taurus often have a sensitive throat and colon. The throat may become infected because of a sluggish colon. The nutritionists may advise that milk or red meats be avoided. A visit to a nutritionist or holistic physician may inspire confidence to change the diet to include the foods you need. It has been said that with this placement the "belly" swells when the diet is incorrect, so a protruding tummy may be the key that diet needs changing. However, all medical diagnoses should be supervised by a professional in the field.

The psychological impact of the father is a difficult one to self-diagnose, for the memories lie hidden in the subconscious mind and only enter the consciousness as a fear or an admonition when you feel the need to confront the world. A strong Saturn placement can inhibit starting new ventures or the development of self worth. For example, a woman with a difficult Saturn placement may feel as though she is a second class citizen because her father treated both her and her mother that way. She may not feel that she has a right to establish a personality. A man with a strong Saturn may feel that he has no right to advance on his job or that he doesn't have the creativity necessary to be successful. He may buckle under any pressure from an authority figure even though he blusters and brags at home.

These periods can be the key to releasing inferiority complexes leaving the personality free to develop to its maximum potential.

• *Uranus-Uranus transits*

This transit is really a cycle. It happens to all of us at some time or another. We experience a complete revolution of Uranus to itself if we live long enough. These cycles will be discussed in another book.

• *Uranus-Neptune transits*

This may or may not be an important transit. Neptune is a generation planet. It indicates the dreams and aspirations of an entire generation. The transit may not have any real effect on your chart, except that we are each born into the world during a certain social period and our generation's social struggle will undergo changes as Uranus works it way through Neptune's sign.

I was born with Neptune in Virgo. As Uranus proceeded through Virgo, many people in this country were affected by a strongly Virgoan ideal. The dream of this generation was to be analytical, technical, critical of the society in which we live and even of each other. When Uranus by transit moved through the sign of Virgo, the country became so preoccupied with technical approaches to life that one had to go to school to learn how to drive a truck! Suddenly you could no longer serve an apprenticeship. Employees were required to be over-trained for most jobs they applied for. The dream of the generation began to manifest.

People who have aspects between Neptune and the personal planets in the natal chart are involved in a different kind of stuggle during a Uranus-Neptune transit, because personal dreams are being activated. Neptune includes clouds of delusion and illusion along with its inspiring energy and the difference between the inspiration and the delusion of the dream needs to be recognized. If the separation between inspiration and delusion is successfully recognized, this transit may indicate a two year period when dreams begin to be fulfilled. The changes in the dream goal can be drastic. The person who has been previously glued to one path may find himself inspired to change direction.

Uranus by transit may even bring a conscious recognition of the goal—it may liberate the dreamy illusion from the recesses of the mind and inspire a person to make the moves necessary in order to manifest the realization of his dream.

• Uranus-Pluto transits

Pluto is another generation planet as many people have a Pluto placement in common. The houses may be different, but the sign will be the same. When Uranus comes along to activate the natal Pluto, the transit becomes important when there are natal aspects between Pluto and the personal planets. Pluto can be called a symbol of the collective unconscious in each of us. It can represent our unconscious motivation. When it is tied to the personal planets, it can indicate that some of our activities or reactions may not be totally inspired by conscious decisions.

When Uranus sets off natal aspects, consciousness can be the result of the two year experience with the transit. Creative energy is often unconsciously motivated. When we learn how to tap into this energy freely, we can produce more. We may develop a broader understanding of what is going on around us. Before we are free to use the creative energy, however, we must muddle through our individual need to control or manipulate our lives or the lives of those who live close to us. The control games we play may have a lot in common with patterns learned from our early childhood environment. Most people who tend to be manipulative or controlling are not motivated by power. More often control games are played by those who feel insecure and the game is played only to increase a feeling of security. However, nothing is secure, and the best laid plans of mice and men sometimes go astray.

As we work with a Uranus-Pluto transit, we may discover that it is easier and much more fun to be free of the need to control. As we continue our games consciously, we become aware of what we are doing, and are thus able to let go of the bad habits. They seldom get us what we want anyway.

• *Uranus Transiting the Angles*

When Uranus transits the angles in the chart, it sets in motion the idea of change as it affects the "cross" of our personality. I feel the transit to the Ascendant is the most important. Because the Ascendant is usually in aspect to the fourth, seventh and tenth house cusps, the major areas of life interest are given attention during this two year period.

First House. Uranus transiting over the Ascendant is similar to that of Uranus transiting the Sun. The Ascendant indicates how we look to other people, how others relate to us, how we put our best foot forward, how we make our new beginnings, the persona that covers the vulnerability of the Sun and the Moon. When Uranus comes within a ten degree orb of the Ascendant, our projections begin to change. We seem different to those who know us.

This energy can be of a highly nervous type, and we may find ourselves becoming easily excited or excitable. We may be more than usually abrupt, we may seem to change our plans on the spur of the moment, and those around us are unsure of our dependability. Uranus indicates the ability to free ourselves, to liberate ourselves from old patterns, old habits, the ruts of the past.

Because the Ascendant relates to our career, we may feel inspired to make changes as to the kind of work we do, or the direction we are moving in. We may make gigantic strides ahead as far as promotions and job offers are concerned.

This transit may indicate changes in lifestyle, career or geographical location as well in relationships. People move from one end of the country to another. They marry or divorce. They end relationships that are no longer productive. They open up to new ideas, new opportunities, new concepts, new people. The energy can be exciting if you are ready for it. Rigid plans will not work out, and any rigid concept of how to begin something will not seem to work as it has in the past. The transit requires that we change. Little will go as scheduled, and the lack of schedule will show up in relationships as well as in the career.

The experiences felt during this transit will usually teach or help the individual undergoing them. Although relationships formed during this time may not be lifelong in duration, they will be beneficial in some way. Any opportunity or new personality opening doors for you during the transit will bring something of value. This transit always gives you some experience you can take with you.

The ill effects of a Uranus transit to the Ascendant usually center around being somewhat accident prone, because the usual care is not taken doing the normal daily functions. It may be wise to be careful driving, leaving plenty of room for error, letting the other driver win, etc. Uranus seems to have something to do with defective machinery, and under hard aspects, you may want to take some extra precautions as long as those precautions don't include paranoia!

The transits gives us a chance to begin to use the higher side or the more constructive qualities of the sign on the Ascendant. It gives us a chance to let go of being overly protective of ourselves. We can become more outgoing.

Fourth House. When Uranus begins to transit the fourth house cusp, it activates the matters governed by the fourth house. This house symbolizes early childhood environment and atmosphere. It indicates what kind of a home we want to create for ourselves as we mature. Uranus coming to the cusp of the fourth indicates an opportunity to better understand how the early environment has affected our adult behavior. It also indicates a probability of changing homes, whether that change is redecorating the home we have, or wanting to move into a new one. Some people move from the city to the country, and country dwellers come to the city.

On a more mundane level, the Uranus transit can indicate a certain amount of accident prone-ness in the home, or some unusual activities taking place around the homefront. Problems that occur because you own your home may have unusual or unorthodox causes or solutions.

Because Uranus signifies liberation, I find that the most important potential coming from the transit is that of liberating the adult from the power of the childhood environment. This takes introspection though, and in order to get the result we have to put some time in on this transit. It doesn't happen by itself.

Seventh House. When Uranus begins to transit the seventh house cusp, it brings several kinds of energy into focus. At the same time it opens up the seventh house, it will be opposing the Ascendant. This means that we will feel our new beginnings are being hampered. We may project this feeling of hampering onto any partner that we may have.

The seventh house indicates what we look for in a marriage or business partner. This transit may signify that partnerships need to change. We usually enter into our marriage relationships in a very similar manner to that of our parents although we don't realize it at the time. If Mom and Dad never had company in the home, it is usually difficult for the child to enter into a relationship where company appears at the door on a regular basis. Any basic pattern that the child absorbed from the parent will be brought into the adult situations in some way, even though the problem or the behavior pattern may seem unimportant to us at the time.

When Uranus goes over the seventh house cusp, we have a chance to liberate ourselves from our parent's concepts so that we can begin to form our own. Our partners may begin to change, forcing us to re-evaluate what we have, or what we expect. If we cooperate with the energy, we may make constructive changes in our lives. If we don't, our partner may become interested in leaving so he or she can make the changes necessary for growth. The personal liberation possible to attain during this period has to do with a more open or more trusting or more comfortable relationship. This may be a time when you are suddenly able to communicate more freely with the person you live with.

Tenth House. When Uranus moves into orb of the tenth house cusp, it begins to bring pressure and activity to what is ruled by the tenth house. Our world image changes, the honors that we reach for from the world begin to change. We may have unexpected opportunitites to "do our thing." We may get unexpected promotions. If we have not been pulling our weight in the business community, we may be let go from a job and it may be a surprise.

The universe cannot give us what we have not earned, so this transit is impossible to predict. Clients are not going to tell you how they have goofed in business. They often come to an astrologer to see if the astrologers "pyschic" powers can give them insight into what can be expected from the future. We don't know how a Uranus transit will work, but if energy has been constructively directed up until this point, the transit should not bring dire distress, but some kind of opportunity.

Because Uranus is so unusual and so unpredictable, I usually talk to clients about accepting all the offers that are made, rather than limiting themselves to only one opportunity. The Uranian energy is so scattered that not all the opportunities will hold water. By accepting all the offers, by "walking on eggs" until the deal comes through, we wind up with something. The person who commits himself to only one opportunity may be left holding the bag, rejecting all the other offers, only to find that the offer he took won't come to manifestation.

Neptune Transits

Neptune travels through the zodiac and dissolves all that we have built up if we don't need it anymore. It softens us. It brings fantasy and delusion into our lives. It changes us in an insidious manner which is hard to recognize. The more rigid types of people become very uncomfortable on this transit, because all the edges of life become fuzzy. It can inspire more solid citizens to drink or take drugs, because those activities further enhance a concept of fantasy. We don't like to cope with the awful reality of feeling out of touch.

Generally speaking, the transit of Neptune seems to be designed to inspire us to let go of certain life patterns and values we no longer need. The transit is nebulous—it's difficult to put your finger on it—it's hard to talk about. It tends to bring a loss of hope or some strange feelings of depression or isolation. It affects our energy level and we may feel guilty because we cannot accomplish what we have in the past. The loss of energy forces us to become more pliable, to find an easier way. The energy is creative as well, so as we learn to let go of old patterns, insights into the development of new methods of handling problems or situations can come to consciousness.

As Neptune transits our various houses, it blinds us to the subject matter that the house symbolizes. We don't see or understand those matters as clearly as we would at other times. We will not have that many houses transited by Neptune in a lifetime and you can see what departments of life will be enlivened or spiritualized by the Neptune contact. Along with the blind spot is a need for us to develop intuition in that area. Neptune both inspires and deludes. Armed with this knowledge, you can see where you will be most apt to be inspired as well as where your are most apt to be gullible.

Fantasy, delusion, loss of hope, a lack of energy, insomnia, tiredness, an inability to concentrate, a lack of goal orientation, all come from the Neptune transit in some way. If the energy is understood, it can be used to develop insight, intuitive ability, inspired action.

• Neptune-Sun transits

When Neptune hits the Sun by transit, the very roots of the personality are shaken, but in a very subtle manner. The Sun symbolizes the self, the "I am" principle, the soul, or the core of personality. It symbolizes vitality, the kind of men in your life, how you cope with authority figures. The hard aspect from Neptune will affect the Sun for a number of *years*. Old concepts and attitudes fade slowly away and will eventually be replaced with new ones. But until the replacement parts come into our consciousness, we feel an insidious draining of our vitality and our values. This feeling can frighten people and it can cause depression as well as a serious loss of hope. the hopelessness will affect different people differently.

The natal aspects to the Sun will be important in understanding this transit, for those aspects will be activated as well. If a person is a destructive type normally, it is possible that he will suffer more during this transit than a person who expresses himself more constructively.

The energy level will appear to be depleted. An individual may think he's anemic only to learn after going to his doctor that he's fine. In order to compensate for the sluggish tired feeling, vitamins may help. Because insomnia is not unusual during the transit, it may be necessary to alter sleeping habits. Often this transit indicates a desire to stay up at night, or an inability to sleep in the evening along with a real desire to take a snooze about two in the afternoon! Obviously, most companies don't support the idea of 2 P.M. snoozes, but taking cat naps in the early evening, or allowing time for sleeping on the weekends won't hurt anyone. Family and friends may not understand the need for sleep, but they'll get used to it. (Part of the Neptune transit's effect is to encourage the removal of unnecessary social obligations!)

The loss of hope attached to the Neptune-Sun transit manifests because the goals, career urges, as well as the will to live, is being nebulously affected. Those people with rigid goals are hurt the most. Some people find the career disappointing, or the work they do seems no longer necessary in the business world. There may be a need for some spiritual involvement, and if the spiritual search is impeded by atheistic ideas or an unpleasant family experience with the more orthodox religions, the door to freedom may be closed. It can be opened. Religious philosophies, the more metaphysical or mystical philosophies will not offer the same barriers that may be presented to the lay members of the average religious order.

This is a period where you are able to see through the veil of illusion and take a good look at some of the more unattractive aspects of business. The loss of hope can become despair at being a part of unsavory business practice. This transit can also indicate a period where the normally careful individual takes chances on a new business venture or a new relationship that doesn't make any sense to those around him.

The hard transits of Neptune to the Sun accomplish a goal in the personality development that is not readily discernable. It requires that we become more conscious. It requires that the spiritual or soul's evolution become conscious. The petty details of the living experience pale because there is just not enough energy to continue with aimless activities that merely kill time. We can survive a loss of hope by developing a new one. But the new one will have to be more universal. Creative energy can come to the fore. A concept of universal consciousness rather than a neighborhood consciousness has a chance to develop.

When you try to forecast Neptune-Sun hard aspects by transit, it's important to consider several factors prior to thinking the worst thoughts possible about the transit. First of all, how old is the client? Are you coupling this particular transit with a mid-life crisis, with young adulthood, with an emotional depression associated with some other life event?

Neptune can hang around a chart for four or five years. If the natal Sun is also in close aspect with other planets in the birthchart, the effect of the transit may last longer. The effect may not be a physically obvious one and may be hard to diagnose—it may even be hard for your client to talk about it. In several instances, because my client was uninterested in hearing anything much about "hope" I just said that it was not unusual to feel a loss of hope especially connected with goals relating to a job. The response was, "Loss of hope, huh?" And several days later a phone call came in with a request for a special appointment to discuss just how Neptune was affecting the chart. Not all people want to hear about Neptune right away. Nevertheless, I try, but subtly. Some clients need to hear about what is going on internally—need to hear that it's okay. Some clients need to hear that it is not abnormal to consider life and death from a philosophical point of view. And I feel strongly aobut allowing the client to examine his life with an eye to dying—for we all usually do it at some time or another.

We first start dealing with our depression sort of like this: "Why am I alive?" or "Why must I stay in this universe—my husband, wife, kids, job, lack of kids, etc., don't really make me happy." We then start to examine our need for happiness. Hopefully, we get to the point where we become more inclusive and begin to wonder why *anything* is alive—the trees, giraffes, other people, etc. We are then on a philosophical road—on the way to developing some ideas about our spiritual or mystical selves, for we are privately examining the nature of our reality. If this individual is exposed to Platonic philosophies or the modern day equivalents, he will work through this transit and be a stronger, more self assured person. He may develop his own personal feelings about spirituality or religion. That's what the transit is there for. If we don't consider our lives and the value of our life, how can we offer anything that is of real value to anyone? Sooner or later we all die, or those we love die—and how can we face that trauma if we haven't confronted our own spirituality?

We can survive this transit without developing one whit of spirituality. We can blunder in and out of new jobs, new careers and new romances. We can feel victimized as we wander aimlessly around being deluded and fooled by the veil of illusion that Maya presents. We can muddle our way through the transit and just be glad it's over, but we've missed something if that's all we did.

Neptune opposed my Sun and Venus when I was a child. Considering my young age along with the fact that I have a twelfth house Sun it wasn't too bad. My parents uprooted me from my neighborhood. They didn't bother to tell me why—I just found myself going on trips to look at houses in the country. I remember vividly one dilapidated farm (victims of the realtor) where cows and chickens were wandering through the open door of a sagging farmhouse that didn't have any windows left in it. My parents wanted to move there? I pondered. We moved to an alien little village in the country—one that had been settled by folks coming over on the Mayflower—and the natives didn't like my parents or me. I was in the school system dealing with the children and my parents weren't. In the process of attempting to make it through each day at the little one room schoolhouse I attended, it never dawned on me to tell my parents what was happening—I had the delusion that they knew! The five year trauma of moving to the country from a surburban neighborhood ties in with the Neptune transit, and when it broke so did the problems. The transit signified a period when I didn't know who I was—I became an alien. It was very disconcerting!

An adult will cope with the energy very differently than a child. A man will handle this transit differently than a woman. The personality center changes. We may not know who we are.

Some astrologers assume that the worst possible events may happen under major transits. For those who worry about children, it might be the time to be more honest and direct with them. A good rapport with a child at this time will help much more than being worried all the time, or expecting the worst to happen. The transit is not meant to destroy us—and we look better as astrologers if we don't engender paranoia in our clients.

• Neptune-Moon transits

The natal Moon symbolizes the feeling response in an individual. It indicates how we nurture and care for what we love. It can indicate how we respond to the mother image or what we learned from the mother image. It can indicate how we respond to life around us. That response can range from how we feel toward a loved one, to our response to politics or poetry. When Neptune comes along by transit, we have four or five years to consider how we are going to change our responsiveness. Our emotional needs may change, and we may feel emotionally vulnerable.

The conjunction, square or opposition are the most difficult, but interesting experiences have also been recorded about the trine. Strange losses can take place during this period. Usually they don't take place until the aspect has worked its way into a three degree orb. I feel that these disasters might be averted if we better understood the point of the transit, for loss and death of loved ones is not the only way to learn about loving.

For some stange reason, emotional bereavement of one kind or another can take place during the hard transits. An insidious or unconventional loss can occcur under this transit—an overdose of drugs, a strange death, a strange ending to a relationship (not unconventional in the sense that Uranus can signify the unconventional but rather an over-reaction to drugs, an undiagnosible disease, an insidious infection, an event that happens between two people that dissolves a relationship). The Maya effect of the Neptune transit comes into play. During a Neptune transit we are constantly coping with a world of illusion.

Philosophically speaking, we create our own world and what we expect we eventually get. Neptune brings a cloud of non-reality. In other words, we don't pay a bit of attention to Mother or Father Nature—we create our own ideals and perhaps our own world. Couple that with Madison Avenue advertising and a few Hollywood movies, and most people have a concept that real life is either covered with gossamer, lace, unearthly beauty, or the blood and gore of violence. In either case, the balance is missing and an unstable base houses our emotional nature.

The Neptune transit is a tool for changing our responses. the basis of our emotional response nature was established in childhood, and now it must change. This is an excellent period for working through childhood images and impressions. It may be a bit difficult for we can also pursue wonderful fantasies and goals. We may become totally involved in people whose motives we cannot see because a cloud of delusion hangs between us and them. We can feel drained of energy and a bit listless. Some people feel so out of sorts they completely avoid relationships for fear of not picking a partner carefully. Others jump into relationships that are mostly molded on fantasy. Some become involved in relationships that exclude sex because they think it isn't spiritual enough.

No matter what we do, we will change as a result of this transit. Our concepts and ideas, our delusions and illusions, our feelings about love and impersonal love will emerge by the end of it.

• *Neptune-Mercury transits*

Mercury symbolizes the manner in which we communicate, so our hearing, speech, thought patterns, touch, taste and smell functions are affected for four or five years when Neptune begins to activate Mercury. Sometimes the transit can last longer, for other aspects to the natal Mercury will also keep it alive.

Neptune brings illusion, delusion and inspiration into the sphere of the mental activities. The energy is insidious—we don't respond to it with "Eureka! I've just discovered atomic energy!" We are drawn to new ideas, strange thoughts and the pursuit of subjects that may have never before held the least interest for us.

If we come from an environment where we have pursued some aspect of the study of self awareness, some kind of therapy that encouraged the process of individuation as Jung described it, this transit will have little effect on us. If we have a background in religion or the study of the mystical side of life, if we are deeply in tune with nature, this transit will not affect us in an overly upsetting manner.

If we have not developed the concept of the inner self, if we are not comfortable with who we are, or with our thoughts, or being "different," we may be in for an unpleasant period. Neptune brings delusion—and part of that delusion may be increased intuition. If a person doesn't know what intuition is, or if he is unfamiliar with what is commonly called e.s.p. he may feel strange and uncomfortable with himself. If the aspects in the natal chart warrant, and if the house placement of Mercury indicates intuitive and psychic ability, this transit may bring intensity involving precognition, precognitive dreams—one may hear voices or see visions or just "know things" before they happen. If this is the case, the transit of Neptune to Mercury (especially the hard aspects, but sometimes the trine) can cause a feeling of instability.

Clients from very "square" or narrowly religious backgrounds have come in for counselling sessions when the transit was in effect. Their common fear was insanity. They were afraid to discuss how they felt. But I said something innocuous like "you should be feeling a bit mentally unstable during this period—or at least you may be worried about it." That opened the door for all kinds of discussion about private fears of going crazy, of becoming completely unstable, of feeling they might not make it.

Neptune brings creativity with it and I firmly believe that this energy can be channeled and put to good use. Instead of being afraid of one's stability, the energy could be used to explore the field of parapsychology, or any area of the occult that seems interesting, including astrology. It can be used for writing, painting, or the pursuit of any creative interest the client may have or for any creative aspect of the job.

The dreams and voices of delusion, coupled with an extreme case of forgetfulness usually serve to make people insecure about things of the mind! Humor helps, for we can adjust to this transit if we have a sense of humor about ourselves. I used to do things like going to the supermarket five times in one day in order to get coffee and buying everything else but that. Finally, in desperation, I talked to the cashier and said, "Don't let me out of here without coffee!" She was undergoing a similar experience for Neptune was also hitting her Mercury which I discovered by doing a quick look in the ephemeris.

We may go from one room to another and when we get there we can't remember what we came for. Or we are driving to a friend's house and end up driving to work or to some other familiar place without realizing where we are. These kinds of activities can upset a person who isn't accustomed to it. Perhaps we can't find things in the office—we don't remember where we filed things.

Sometimes communications are really muddled and we misunderstand what others are telling us or we are unclear about what we are trying to communicate to those around us. All this serves to unsettle our self image of capability. The more unsettled and uncomfortable we get, the more we add to any feeling of inadequacy. The trick is to learn how to apply this same befuddled energy to creative, meditative thinking.

• Neptune-Venus transits

When this one hits you for four or five years, you will slowly and subtly learn something about changing your concept of what love means to you. Most of us have a pie-in-the-sky attitude about love—it is some wonderful, illusory feeling experience that is charming but often impractical. Even under the trine aspect we can get into wonderful delicious trouble! We fall in love with love, we fall in love with an ideal, with a spiritual ethic, with a cloud, or under one. Since Venus symbolizes our intellectual concept of what love is and how we appreciate being loved, and it also has some symbolic tie to the psychological impact of our early experience with the mother and her values early in our lives, all these aspects of personality are bound to change under this transit.

The most common occurance during the transit is that of falling in love with someone who we can't really relate to for a long period of time. Men fall in lvoe with captivating women who appeal to them, but the personality profile of the male doesn't agree with the kind of relationship he's presently involved in. For example, the business executive who needs time and freedom to pursue his business dealings falls in love with an insecure clinging vine who needs constant attention and supervision. And she may be pressuring him into marriage.

Or a woman falls in love with potential and doesn't see *who* she has fallen in love with. Women are sometimes drawn to creative men who don't work, who are irresponsible, who are not what they seem. Guilt may manifest in both sexes under this transit for there seems to be some need or obligation to prove how spiritual and how much they are in love by marrying their loved one, sometimes faster than necessary. Along with Neptune delusion goes a change in the spiritual urges. Mere sex, or mere gratification, or mere emotion, is not what this individual is looking for. The Neptune influence inspires the great "spiritual" love that is above that of ordinary mortals. Either party in the relationship may press the need for a marriage contract or some special commitment that will prove to either of the lovers that this is not the ordinary relationship, but rather one made in heaven.

The transit indicates a search for that which is beyond the realm of the ordinary. There is nothing wrong with searching for a special relationship that also includes a spiritual tie. But the delusion that Neptune brings comes into play here, and this transit indicates a time when friendships can be invaluable, for your friends may see what you can't. Parents, friends, neighbors, your local astrologer, chart comparisons and composites are all a help. We may not listen anyway, but the help is there if we want it. The love we search for will be there when the transit is out. In the meantime, what's wrong with checking his finances? Does either partner have IRS problems or a good work history? Do you really have anything in common beside this wonderful spiritual attraction? We are searching so intensely for a special relationship that we may be manufacturing it in our fantasies, thinking we have it when we really don't.

Some people lose all interest in relationships under this transit, for the fantasy and the dream of a perfect relationship makes those that might happen in the real world rather disenchanting to say the least. Some people who have been apprehensive about reaching out to love someone will kick over the traces and take a chance on getting involved on this transit. The normal barriers are let down, and the desire nature, or the need for love may be more easily expressed. Obviously, this will happen to a person who has a heavily afflicted Venus at birth, and who would normally be quite cautious about emotional commitments.

Knowing your chart, and knowing your natal aspects will help you through this transit. Some common sense will help as well. The more practical considerations of a relationship may solve all your involvement problems. If you want to get married and have a family, the alcoholic or the unemployed don't help much unless you like to suffer. Thinking about the kind of companion you need will help you keep your feet on the ground. And talking to your best friends will give you a clue as to what they find offensive about your new love. Although we don't like to hear this kind of conversation from a friend, we may need to listen during this transit. As I mentioned earlier, my mother used to say, "Don't make love by the garden gate, 'cause love is blind but the neighbors ain't." She was talking about the fact that other people see what we refuse to look at. We are important enough to carefully consider our needs before commiting ourselves to long term relationships that aren't what they seem. Anyone who wants us to prove how much we love them may have motives we don't presently understand.

• Neptune-Mars transits

Mars represents the "I act" principle and governs the actions we take when we express the needs of the Sun. It also symbolizes the sex drive of both men and women. As Neptune transits this point, especially under the hard aspects, our concept of action changes. We may not know what we are doing! Neptune brings insidious energy. In other words, it subtly and slowly draws energy away, and this can make us seem disorganized and forgetful. As far as the sex drive is concerned, it changes that as well.

If Mars is in a powerful sign, or if it is well aspected, it may adjust the sex drive in some way. Those with a low profile sex drive may have a lower one or perhaps no sex drive at all. Those with an inhibited sex drive may become more prone to fantasy at this time as Neptune indicates our fantasies, our dreams, our illusions and delusions, and our inspiration as well. So suddenly, the sexuality factor becomes more prone to fantasy. Some people want to act out their fantasies, some are afraid of them. Because Mars is the action principle, certain signs will have less energy.

We don't like anything to interfere with our sex drive as we are often quite sensitive about it. When disinterest in sex occurs, when a woman becomes no longer interested in sharing herself physically with her partner, or when a man finds himself feeling impotent, people can get pretty distressed! The sex drive is changing; the values are becoming more spiritual.

One male client was in his early thirties and single when this transit occurred. He proceeded to jump in bed with every lady he could find, looking for something special that he couldn't name. But none of the sex was special enough. He was also having potency problems and as the tension mounted, the sex became more and more disappointing. The Neptune transit is an internal one and he didn't understand that. He needed to change his values about sexuality. He seemed to have a lot of sexual guilt that may have been caused by his early religious training, and that influence needed to be consciously understood. His own need for indiscriminate sexual activity and inability to maintain a relationship even for short periods of time, was what really needed to be looked at. He was reaching outside of himself for answers at a time when he should have been looking within. The disappointment that he felt should have caused some internal changes in how he viewed sex.

If the natal chart warrants it, this transit can be indicative of someone retreating into fantasy rather than taking action on an outer plane. If Mars also aspects the Sun or the Moon, or even the Ascendant, the presentation of this individual (the Ascendant) or the spiritual (Sun) or emotional needs (Moon) are affected by the transit. The energy becomes more complicated and involves a larger chunk of the personality. This can indicate a time of daydreaming, of visualization, of meditation colored with fantasy. Not only are the fantasies sexual in nature, they can also involve a large fantasy—that of the life process.

Mars was the ancient ruler of Scorpio, the sign of death, destruction and *regeneration*. The sperm or the "seed" symbolizes the life that is a part of us. It is not consciously engendered by any of us—we have it. The life force, either the giving birth to a child, or providing the semen to give it life is symbolized by the Hindu god figure Shiva. He is the Lord of Death, Destruction and Regeneration. He dances the dance of life and death, and while he dances the sperm just flows and flows but his upper torso is feminine. Not all renditions of Shiva include this imagery—but his is a glorious dance of life and death. It is not the destructive fear of death, but the continuity of life, the universal flow which is symbolized by his dance. And it is difficult for westeners to understand.

The Neptune-Mars transit includes thinking about the continuity of life—the life force that once was symbolized by Mars. Even though the symbolism of astrology has changed, and even though Scorpio has a different ruler today, and even though many astrologers only see Mars as negative or malefic—the beat goes on. Under a Mars-Neptune transit, we wonder what life is all about.

Some people don't wonder. Some people cope with the inability to function sexually, and create a lot of tension for themselves. Some feel that you must live out your fantasies for that is a part of being "free." Sometimes people are able to overcome serious blocks in expressing sexuality during this period, for the walls of Saturnian caution are thrown to the winds, and the personality has a chance to express itself. However, a balance needs to be created, for it's hard to live with too much promiscuity as a part of one's past. One thing that can be learned from too many flings is that sex only becomes what each of us wants it to be. We make it as special or as humdrum as we wish.

The transit should be considered in terms of the client's *age*. A single girl of twenty-five, living in New York City away from her parents, might do some sexual experimentation on this one. A married woman or forty-five may have an affair, but she may also re-evaluate her relationship with her husband. The transit's effect on a more mature person will depend a great deal on how much she values her past. She may have a fling—but she may stay with her husband too. A man will respond much in the same way—he may react very differently to the Neptune energy if he is a part of a healthy relationship than if he is footloose and fancy free.

A teenager can only respond in terms of his age. I experienced a square from Neptune to my natal Mars when I was in high school in the fifties. It was not socially acceptable to "fool around," but I had wonderful fantasies about what sex would be like if I ever did it. And necking was a wonderful experience. And gothic novels were read by the dozens! Had I been born later, my parents may have had a lot more cause to worry, but my generation and environment were safe for me.

In today's social structure, parents might want to be more aware of these transits. Some parents project too much on their children however, and take little notice of how developed their children are. Even if a Neptune-Mars transit is affecting a teenage girl, she will not respond sexually unless she is ready. Many teenagers are not ready to experiment with sex even though their parents worry that they are. Warm and compassionate education is the key here.

• *Neptune-Jupiter transits*

We now begin to get away from the really personal planets when we consider Neptune transiting natal Jupiter. Jupiter symbolizes our ability to relate, our ability to exchange ideas and values with other people. It indicates how we open up to people, to new experience, to new ideas. Neptune brings a subtle influence and our ideas of expansion and sharing become more spiritual...or more nebulous. We relate in an inspirational, delusional, illusional, fantasmal, or ethereal manner. It can be a wonderful transit for helping us to open up.

The pitfalls come when we don't know who we are relating to, or if we open up in a totally indiscriminating manner. And if we do, Saturn will come along and eventually straighten everything out. We will see the error of our ways sooner or later!

Jupiter has been traditionally associated with tumors and the like, sometimes with glandular infections. Anytime Neptune transits a planet, it tends to cloud the issue, to veil and cover the reality of what is going on underneath. Under this transit it may be a good idea to check out preventive medicine. It may be difficult to get motivated to see the doctor, for Jupiter also has something to do with rich food and goodies so people may go off diets, or eat too much junk food, or drink too much alcohol. It tastes so good going down.

The transit will be as important as is indicated in the natal chart. If Jupiter is heavily aspected to the personal planets, this will be a time of changes in attitude. Rigidity will dissolve, and anything that needs to be dissolved in your life will dissolve. Energy flow may not be what it should be or what it has been before. In order to compensate for the tired feeling, you may have to change the way you relate. The house activated by the transit will be more important than usual.

This is a good period to test whether or not your personal philosophy holds any water. In order to attain the most consciousness, we have to discover the content of our Jupiter-Saturn symbolism. Neptune dissolves the dreams and the delusions of our philosophical nature, and allows us to replace them with even better ones. The thing to keep in mind is that we must have a philosophy that works—that we can live seven days a week. If we can't live it, we don't have one.

• *Neptune–Saturn transits*

Neptune transits dissolve something. Saturn represents many things in the natal chart, and any one of these facets of personality may be changed during the Neptune transit. Saturn indicates what we are cautious about by its house, sign and aspects. What we regard with caution is that which we are somewhat afraid of—either externally or internally. The Saturn placement indicates the smallest or least developed function of the body. Some astrologers interested in health say that Saturn in Cancer, for example, indicates difficulties with digestion. Under a Neptune transit, this part of the body may "act up."*

Saturn can also symbolize the psychological affect of the father on the child's psyche. This imprint occurs during the formative years prior to the age of three. If this affect causes blocks about authority figures or blocks normal interests or development, it will be shown by the additional aspects to Saturn in the natal chart. Under a Neptune transit, some of these blocks may surface and dissolve. This can free the individual to take his place in society on his own terms. He can free himself of restrictive family influence.

The Neptune transit, whether in a conjunction, square or an opposition to natal Saturn, will begin to dissolve some of the fears and cautions in the personality. This dissolution allows each person to look at his cautions differently, with a new attitude. If Saturn indicates a lack of self-worth, for example, this transit may help begin to build one. The individual coping with a self-worth problem may see that he *has* worth, even if he only realizes how well he handles his job. He may begin to see he has value as a friend, as a tax-payer, as an employee, as a neighbor. No matter where the concept of self-worth begins, the dissolving energy of Neptune allows this person to set aside cautions long enough to begin to see himself in society.

If the chart indicates really strong ties to the father, those kinds of ties that make it difficult to break away from family influence, this transit may indicate a period of negative response to the family. It is a reaction to breaking away from the father's power and his affect on the child's personality. We can move five hundred miles from home and bring all his influence with us, for the influence of Saturn is one that is carried in the subconscious. The real life father may have no idea that his child responds to him the way he does. But the child is left with the need to work out the subconscious influence, and the problem is difficult when the influence isn't expressed or known. Under a Neptune–Saturn transit, the young adult may jump into some activity that could later be diagnosed as a form of rebellion against the family. The probability of the young adult seeing his activity as rebellion is slim.

*See *Medical Astrology and Health* by William M. Davidson. Dr. Davidson did a series of nine lectures about medical astrology as it relates to homeopathy. The lectures can be obtained from the Astrological Bureau, 5 Old Quaker Rd., Monroe, N.Y. 10950.

When this transit hits at a later age, the rebellion may be even more subtle. It may represent itself as a marriage to a person the family doesn't approve of. It may represent itself as a pulling away from everything that was previously valued by the father. An interest in a different business may emerge. This may also indicate a time when a seemingly complacent married person leaves one spouse and becomes involved with a totally different kind of partner. Whatever the father impressed upon his child as important will change as the child begins to free himself from the influence of the family and begins to create a life of his own.

The key to working with this transit seems to come from the internal changes going on within. Suddenly we find ourselves interested in doing something we never thought we could do before. We never thought we were capable of handling whatever it is, and the fears seem to evaporate just long enough for us to get started, and we find out that we can do it! Once the initial change is made, we can take our energy flow as far as we wish.

• Neptune-Uranus transits

This transit is a generational one, that is, it happens to everyone who is born around the same year. Unless Uranus is aspected to the personal planets in the natal chart, the transit may not be eventful. We will notice our generation changing rather than personal changes.

In the natal chart, Uranus indicates the behavior of our generation. Neptune will change this behavior somewhat. We may find that we must change with the times. We must change the way we behave and the pattern of our lives in order to keep up with present day circumstances. If our behavior has been too eccentric or too willful in the past, Neptune will insidiously show us that we must give in to the larger consciousness. Old life styles disappear from under us, leaving us to figure out what happened. If we have been doing our own thing exclusively, we may find that it becomes necessary to join a group, or to change our pattern to conform with the needs of others. It can leave a person feeling that he has been "had" by the universe, without having any clear definition of what it was that got him.

Uranus signifies your personal need for individuation and the Neptune transit can indicate the timing for this kind of interest to develop. This may be the period of years when people explore the world of philosophy, or religion, meditation, or the various kinds of therapies that help one discover inner potential. Or you may see nothing at all happening in the chart.

When Uranus aspects the personal planets, the Neptune transit will dissolve some of the conflicts. For example, should someone have a natal Uranus-Venus square, the Neptune transit may soften the natal tendency to jump to conclusions. The Neptune-Venus transit would also be in effect, and the natal aspect would be activated. This may be a period when this individual can comprehend, or feel, or be more compassionate about this side of his personality. He may begin to realize how his behavior affects others. He may begin to dissolve the habit pattern that causes his reactions to love.

Because Neptune moves so slowly, this will be a facet of personality that changes slowly as well. It is not a transit that comes and gets you, but it will slowly work at the dissolution of old problems.

• Neptune-Neptune transits

These activities are really cycles in the evolution of a personality and will not be discussed here.

• Neptune-Pluto transits

Because both Neptune and Pluto are planets that involve generations of people, the personal effect of any Neptune transit on your Pluto may not be noticeable. If Pluto ties into the personal planets in the natal chart, this transit suddenly becomes important but more so because of the other planets involved. Pluto symbolizes the unconscious motivation of a generation, and of a person, especially as you look to the house placement and aspects. Pluto can indicate control needs or the need to manipulate others. If Pluto is afflicted in the natal chart, you'll begin to see how this person was trained to react to certain life experience, and the training will have come from one or both of the parents. As Pluto ties into the natal planets, it can be better interpreted during a Neptune transit. Neptune will help disssolve some of the control urges. This may be a period of years when those needs can be finally understood and let go. We all know that we can't "make" anyone love us or want us, etc., and under this transit we can become more high-minded. It's really important to understand the Pluto function in the natal chart, so this transit can be used beneficially. For that I would recommend that you consult various astrologers and their work on Pluto. My opinions are voiced in *Astrological Insights into Personality,* published by Astro-Computing Services, 1980.

● *Neptune transiting the Angles*

Neptune hitting the angles will only liven up the facets of life that are ruled by the angular houses. All of the angles may be activated at the same time during the Neptune transit. Like the other transits, I feel that the Neptune-Ascendant transit is the most important.

First House. The most difficult transit from Neptune to the Ascendant is the conjunction. The square and opposition may bring difficulty as well, but the square will emphasize the fourth or tenth houses and the opposition will involve the seventh. The Ascendant represents how you "put your best foot forward," so to speak. It symbolizes the masquerade that we present, and it can be used to understand how we appear to others, how we function at the career level, how we begin things.

When Neptune conjuncts the Ascendant, we really don't know what we are doing. We may look vague and preoccupied to others—sometimes doctors even think our glazed look means we're on some kind of drug. We may simply be under a Neptune transit! We may not know where we are going, or where we have put things. We may lose money. We may have little perspective. We may start new ventures with a devil-may-care attitude, not really checking out what our new responsibilities are—we may take big chances with our career.

The energy level is affected, much like Neptune transiting the Sun or Moon. We may be constantly tired, or we may be unable to sleep when we should. Some people feel guilty about not being able to accomplish what they have planned. The transit requires that we learn how to use our energy differently, as we don't have time to become immersed in all the petty details that we have been previously able to play with.

The transit brings creativity with it, but we may be listening to the beat of a different drummer, or we may not be comfortable expressing our new ideas because they seem so different.

This is not a great period for diagnosing what a career should be, and it can be hard on the young person trying to decide on a college major. Some people marry under this transit, not really realizing what he or she is getting into. Some people pursue unrealistic goals. Eventually, the transit passes. You may have trouble trying to advise a client on this one, for most people don't listen. Because Neptune rules film and delusion, this can sometimes indicate that the starstruck should pursue the career.

The main issues about transiting Neptune are the development of the intuitive ability and the process of dissolution. As we develop our intuitive ability we don't trust the inner voice. Because of a trial and error process, the astute individual can begin to learn how to trust the inner voice—usually the hard way. This is the experience gained by, "I should have listened to my inner self," and after enough experiences at not listening we begin to trust the intuitive process.

The dissolving effect of Neptune brings experience that takes away—we lose something. One of the basic losses is that of physical energy. How can we get where we wish to go without it? We must learn a new way. We must cut through the cultural dross and come to the point. If we remain immersed in trivia, we cannot become in touch with the creative energy within. Just being too tired to "play the game" can help us develop a new outlook.

Fourth House. Most of you already know what I'm going to say about the fourth house. To me it symbolizes the effect of the early childhood environment. The sign on the fourth house cusp tells you the atmosphere of the early home. For those people who wish to explore memories of early childhood, the Neptune transit can be beneficial because it sharpens the intuitive ability and allows us to cut through the patterns of adult consciousness in order to remember the past. The point of looking back on early childhood is not to blame the parents for hurting us but to free ourselves from the bonds of the past.

This transit opens us up to new ideas that we may have never encountered or even thought of before. The transit usually forms a square to the ascendant, also forcing us to make some changes in the way we present ourselves because we just don't have the energy to maintain old patterns.

In a mundane sense, the transit can symbolize a period of time when you may wish to be more cautious about what you allow to go on in your home. You may find that your present homefront is the place where you are most easily deluded. If your intuition tells you that something is going on, you are probably right. Like when your teenage son swears he wasn't smoking pot in his room—yeah, kid. But keep on the alert, because you may be right.

Seventh House. This is an interesting transit to watch, although it doesn't seem to be too interesting to live. Here the partnerships you have begin to change, and you may not see the writing on the wall. Quite a few clients have had relationships dissolve on this one and they can't seem to relate to where the partner is coming from. So far, I haven't seen this kind of ending of a relationship as bad—for it has been coming on for years. The relationship ended years ago, and the couple was staying together for convenience. They each had separate interests, and each seemed to have outside love interests as well. But in all cases that I have dealt with, my clients didn't want to end the relationship or even face the fact that it was over. This may be happening because Neptune is also opposing the Ascendant when it conjuncts the seventh house cusp. So my clients didn't really know what they were doing either. It's a confusing time, for no one is making any sense. When we go through a difficult transit, it's nice to have a sensible partner around to help us straighten out, and during this transit, your partner is no better off than you are.

Because Neptune dissolves things in strange ways, I would venture that this transit indicates the end of something that needs to end in order that you change your perspective. After the pain is over, a new life can start to develop. In my experience, this transit has not brought death, but rather strange endings, strange separations.

Tenth House. When Neptune gets to the conjunction of the tenth house cusp, it brings with it all kinds of illusion and delusion as to what the world image or the public image should be. This is a bit tricky to interpret. Usually I recommend that my clients follow their dream. Neptune brings illusion and delusion, and it also signifies a time in life when we stop looking at reality and start chasing a dream. It may be wise to listen to what the dream is about before you dump cold water on it. All things being equal, if your client isn't looking to see his children starve to death while he goes off on some ridiculous business venture that even you as the astrologer can determine is absolutely ridiculous, he should do it. Some of my clients have reached out for fame and fortune and they have gotten it under this one. However, you can't reach out if you aren't prepared to offer anything—you have to do your homework, offer the universe what it needs, and give it with gusto.

Pluto Transits

Pluto moves very slowly, although it has been gathering momentum these last few years, and people are now experiencing Pluto cycles at an earlier age than they did before. In the natal chart, Pluto has been used to indicate the unconscious motivation or drive of a generation and how that drive may affect people born in certain time periods. It has also been used to ascertain how much of a need there is to manipulate or control the life experience or one's associations with people.

The underlying cause for control urges is a need for "safety." People with strong control needs, or people who maintain a manipulative life style are usually those who were taught that it was necessary to create an environment that was safe. Sometimes these ideas come from a strong tie to the images of the collective unconscious as it is described by Jung. This theory basically rejuvenates the psychic or mythic images of different societies that form our various pasts. Because contemporary societies have strayed so far from accepting universal images into our present living experience, certain people feel strong urges to place controls or stops on the outer environment in order to have some say over what is happening on an inner, mythic level. We often suppress our dreams. We have little outlet in contemporary religious symbolism; our philosophical, mythic, or religious symbolism is covered by a pragmatic outlook. We as a species have almost forgotten that we *are* a species. After many years of oblivion, and with the help of Jung's work, many of those in the field of psychology or comparative religion are reviving interest in such matters as dreams, intuition, the world soul.

On the one hand, we all rationally understand that we have no control over the future, but nonetheless, we attempt to control our future by insuring our relationships and looking for safety in the relationships we indulge in. What irony—we know, yet we don't believe it! It's similar to those who cast aspersions on astrology and run to an astrologer as soon as trouble hits. We all need to move forward, but we can't seem to leave our past.

The Pluto transit helps us to do just that. It helps us or, rather, it *forces* us to let go. It seems that the recently discovered planets (Uranus, Neptune, and Pluto) help us develop a more universal consciousness. It's almost as though these planets were waiting to be discovered as the world became more complicated. Spiritual astrologers say that we are entering the Aquarian age, that we are developing more understanding and a higher consciousness than those who have gone before. If this is so, it seems that the generation planets provide the energy and the impetus to help us increase our awareness of how to live with many different kinds of people and situations on a planet that is getting smaller and smaller because of a change caused by modern technology. Several generations ago it was possible to live and die in one small town without ever being touched by a larger universe. Today that privacy is no longer possible, and if you can read a paper or if you own a television set, you are suddenly aware of the plight of people with whom you may never have to come into contact. This requires a great deal of tolerance for we begin to be confronted by peoples whose culture and living habits are vastly different than ours. The separation of cultures is lessening and an age where we all speak the same language is on its way. The transits of the outer planets push each of us in a different way to become more open to the change.

These changes do not mean that the world is going to become friendly and mature in the next twenty years! But as we learn to deal with our control needs, as we learn to trust the inner intuitive self, we may find it less and less necessary to set up rigid barriers that seemingly protect us. If we don't want to become extinct like the dinosaur, we need to learn to change as the world changes—and those who can't or won't will become relics. Pluto says change—let go of the past; accept the transformation that is at hand. The change may not be universal, but it certainly can be meaningful.

• *Pluto–Sun transits*

The Sun symbolizes the "I am" principle in each of us. It symbolizes the traits and qualities of self that we will use and learn about in a lifetime.

The aspects to the natal Sun indicate the blocks and credits that we bring with us, and the house placement will indicate which department in life holds special emphasis. When Pluto comes along, we have to *let go* of our rigid patterns and forms of expression in order to transform and let the process of individuation develop as much as possible.

A conjunction, square or opposition from Pluto to the Sun is not an easy transit to live through but you can do it, for many have! The Cardinal signs have been coping with it as of late, for Pluto is presently transiting the sign of Libra, forming an opposition to certain degrees of Aries, and a square to certain degrees of Cancer and Capricorn. No matter what the Sun sign may be, Pluto eventually comes along and and brings its own special set of circumstances that we need to learn how to handle.

In my own case, I was dealing with the opposition. For a number of years, I had been working to establish myself in my field by doing a certain kind of work with my clients and students. At the same time, I was accustomed to getting a certain amount of work done in a certain amount of time, and I was old enough to have a pretty good idea of what could be accomplished in a week without exhausting myself.

At the beginning of the Pluto transit, I began to notice that no matter how hard I worked, I wasn't getting anywhere. The astrology textbooks didn't have any answers as to how to expect the energy to manifest, except that astrologers generally said that you might feel a loss of control, or that one might get "done in" under Pluto. It was a transit to be feared. I couldn't get involved in the fear approach, for I believe that the universe gives back what we put into it, and if we have not been involved in wrongdoing, we should not be unseated under a Pluto transit. I began to talk with others born at early degrees of the Cardinal signs, trying to understand what the general prognosis was in regard to the Pluto energy.

Pluto rules Scorpio, the sign of death and regeneration, as well as of transformation. The Pluto transit should then bring some of the transformative possibilities of Scorpio into our environment. And the other side of Pluto, the controlling, noncooperative energy that can manifest is also a side of Scorpio in a less evolved stage—that of "Do as I say do and not as I do do." During the period when Pluto opposed my Sun (using a ten degree orb), a period of about five years, for Pluto went retrograde and direct, I found that I was in the process of a heavy personal transformation.

Many of the beliefs I held since childhood had to be re-evaluated. I began to pull myself up from my roots, so to speak, and the childhood ideals about life, womanhood, work, friendships, relationships and what to expect from all this had to change. Many times I didn't like what the changes signified. The realities that I had to face were unpleasant, but I began to learn about what is rather than what should be.

As far as work was concerned, the more exact Pluto became in the opposition, the more frustrating work became. Not that I didn't like what I was doing—far to the contrary. The problem was that so much work was coming in, and so many people were asking for a piece of my time, that the days weren't long enough to handle the promises. There were periods of hysteria because obligations were calling and they were impossible to fulfill. So many things needed doing that I became short-tempered when I saw precious time being wasted with trivia. Unfortunately, people involved with trivia seldom realize it, so some hurt feelings were left behind until I began to realize that others didn't have the schedule or the transit I had!

Patterns were uprooted and familiar habits and ideas had to be shelved or buried as they were dead. The realization that old values were gone was heart breaking on occasion, for some of the things that had to be given up were precious. Old relationships began to crumble, and some of them hurt when they went. It became obvious that some relationships were not formed on the bonds of friendship, but rather something else, and the reality of that knowledge is never pleasant to face. It became important to form relationships where communication was open, where thoughts could be shared, and under this transit one becomes more sensitive to what is going on beneath the surface, similar to the qualities of Scorpio.

A tremendous change in perspective can take place during this transit. The change may not be obvious to others because it involves your innards and not your outer manifestation. If you are working with the energy to the best of your ability, if you are looking to establish a new path, if you are trying to read the signals on the map you have been given, the transit doesn't really hurt. If you don't see any of the signals and you don't want to change, you may find yourself in the middle of a pickle, or you may find yourself being used or placed in tacky situations by those you considered to be your friends and allies. However, the universe gives you plenty of time to see the writing on the wall if you look for it.

People in business find they must change the way it is being handled. All kinds of subversive activity can take place now. If the business is in the hands of others who run it for you, you may want to spot check to learn whether or not the job is being done. Employees may be undermining you. The energy requires that a change take place, that you uproot some of your "old ways" to make room for the new ones that need to get underway. Some companies branch out at this time, because they are looking for ways in which to keep up with the current trends and the needs of the people as they continue to change.

You may feel you are that mouse on the proverbial treadmill, running around and around and never getting anywhere. At the end of the day the same situations that were there in the morning are still there and nothing has been cleared up. The pressure is intense but *subtle*. A Saturn transit is easy to work with, for it is easily discernible—the frustrations are concrete and obvious. *Pluto transits are not obvious.* They are based on inner changes rather than on outer ones. It can feel like you are walking in a swamp with no dry land under your feet; it can feel like you are about to step into the abyss but you can't talk about it because no one will understand what you are saying. People you talk with may try to dismiss you as a neurotic or a "'worrier." In the midst of the loneliness of being on your hero venture alone, tremendous inner changes are taking place.

Under this transit, for the first time in my life, I was able to understand the expression, "Give yourself up to God. " It doesn't matter what your God is in this instance. For many years, I've believed that each human being possesses a piece of the original creative essence that formed the world—not just each human being, actually, but every formed thing in the universe has creative essence whether it knows it or not and whether it uses it or not. I feel that within the depths of my being there is a piece of that creative essence that leads me in the direction that I am meant to go. Under this transit, it was necessary that I learn how to call on it, to ask that part of myself for guidance and direction for my life was changing. I knew it was changing, but I had no idea of what the outcome would be.

If you are moving in the right direction for yourself, you will survive the Pluto transit. Those who are moving in unhealthy directions will encounter great difficulty and the world will seem to drop out from under them. Old or previously stable relationships will end and careers will change drastically. If your direction is right, it will get shaken and altered because it needs to be redirected. Events will take place around you and you will have to handle them, but the events will not happen to you. You can be lifted out of patterns that have been established for many years, and re-birth yourself into a completely different lifestyle. All the time the transit is taking place, it may be wise to keep looking for that change in direction, so you can get on the bandwagon voluntarily rather than being forced on it.

Letting go of the past is difficult for most people. There are some minor things that can be done to help the transit get started. The cellar, the attic and the closets in most of our homes hold collections of the past. These items and memories need to be cleaned out. It sparks something in the psyche when we do this—almost as if we are telling the inner self to let go. It helps the consciousness to let go as well. The pipes and the plumbing are sometimes affected, so be ready for plumbing repairs. If you live in an apartment, the landlord will do the work, but be ready for the leaks springing up. And if you own a car, you'll have some activity with tailpipes and mufflers! My tailpipes were stolen twice during the transit! But that's minor stuff.

Pluto has something to do with pipes and sewage—so be glad your own internal sewage system is working okay. And under a Pluto transit to either the Sun or the Moon, it may be wise to check into any intestinal infection. Some clients have had trouble ridding themselves of usually minor infections like the flu because Pluto seems to "heat up" everything it touches, and causes bacteria in the body to reproduce faster than normal. Some people are more prone to venereal diseases during this period, and the vulnerability would apply to both Sun and Moon afflictions by transiting Pluto. One might even be careful when it hits Venus or Mars. We don't want to become hypocondriacs but it is wise to stay on top of these kinds of infections rather than letting them get out of hand.

When several aspects are hitting at once, and one of the transits is a strong Pluto transit, you might advise a little caution. Attempts made to control the universe might not work. The dangerous ski slope, the too long swim, the over-endurance number might not be recommendable at this time.

My only experience with danger on this one involved my car on a highway late at night. I was pushing again—trying to get home so I could get some more work done the next day. I was traveling near my home when the electrical system failed on the car, necessitating a tow. Mars by transit was also activating some rough natal aspects, and the tow truck driver became very threatening. I was stranded fifteen minutes out of New York City and it took me over four hours to get home. I was on two dead end roads, and the driver was telling me that he was almost out of gas and he was looking for some. But when we finally got into New York I asked him if he had enough gas to get home, and he informed me he had almost a full tank! A truck, no less! You drivers will know that a truck holds a lot of gas. This man drove through deserted sections in Newark until I confronted him and asked just exactly what was he up to. I felt that he had some unhealthy intentions and hadn't really formulated a plan—I didn't know if he planned to rob me, rape me or kill me. Or maybe he was just gone on drugs and didn't know what he was doing. At any rate, he cheated me of fifteen dollars and scared me half to death. And I said to the universe, "Uncle!" That was the end of my pushing schedules. I gave up and let go. From then on, I did what I could with each day—I gave it my best and that was all I could do. The tension was gone. I realized that I had learned my lesson.

• *Pluto-Moon Transits*

The Moon indicates our emotional nature. It can symbolize the role our mother played in a physical sense, when we were small children and were open to absorbing from her. We learn how to respond to the world around us from our contact with the early mother-child period. The house placement and sign of the Moon will tell something about how we respond, and to what area of life we respond with the most sensitivity. Our ideas of nurturing and warmth come from the Moon's sign as well as our inner motivation for affection. When Pluto comes along by transit to conjunct, square or oppose the Moon, our emotional nature is being uprooted in some way. Perhaps this is a time when we are able to become more conscious of our feelings and intuitive abilities.

Most people react poorly to Moon/Pluto transits, for the emotional nature is being uprooted and changed, and we don't really feel sure of how we will respond to the stimulii from the universe around us. We may overreact to situations thrust upon us. Our emotional reactions may be socially unacceptable. We may not be sure of how we will respond and therefore attempt to put a tight rein of control on every reaction.

The Pluto transit will be there for about five years working slowly on the emotional nature, and giving us all plenty of time to absorb and accept the changes going on within. The energy becomes more intense as the orb gets within five degrees of the Moon. And aspects to the natal

Moon will be incorporated into the complexity of the transit. The more complex the transit, the greater the subtle tension and anxiety that manifests as the transformation takes place. People who have advance warning that this growth is occurring will obviously have less trouble with it, for the need to place controls on the emotional reactions is alleviated, and the person is free to explore the possibility of change within herself.

The changes are *emotional* and not rational. The emotional nature is uneasy and uncomfortable because responses are changing, so most of us make valiant attempts to control our emotions. This control need may be demonstrated when we approach every emotional response so carefully that we look like robots. We create some of the tension because we hold in our responses and it becomes tiring. If we are afraid to overreact in the office, every work problem becomes a trauma we try to hide. We may overreact to employers or co-workers, seeing normal business situations as gigantic crises rather than taking them in stride.

In a personal sense, we want to know where we stand and we become cautious about personal relationships. We may become unsure of a partner and begin to look for too much security. If we are not attached to anyone, relationships may be formed with lovers who are controllable types—those people who need you too much. The Pluto transit may entice us to choose a less than adequate partner in order to insure our security.

When Pluto hits the natal Moon of a child, the symptom will not be the same as it would be for an adult. My Moon was afflicted at birth, and when the Pluto transit conjuncted the natal Moon, I experienced a lot of violence. The violence came from both the neighborhood children and Mother Nature. There was no real way my parents could have known of the danger, and some would blame it on my Sun sign. During the time of Pluto transiting my Moon, Neptune was also opposing my Sun and Venus. Parents can help children through periods like this if they know what is happening astrologically. We moved into a strange neighborhood, one that didn't appreciate my foreign born parents. I suppose the Neptune transit clouded my judgement but I was totally surprised that the local children would not accept me...or my parent's strange accent. One day I was invited to play with some neighboring children and they tried to throw me off a roof of a barn. I was saved because the kid's mother came out of the house at exactly the right time. Physical accidents took place like driving over a cliff in a tractor and falling into an old well. Animals that I loved died and I was exposed to the concept of death. Death and violence is a part of growing up, but it has less effect on a child who is not also being effected by the outer planets.

Teenagers experiencing this transit in a city may be more exposed to unattractive sexuality than children in the country. These children may also experience violence if the Moon is afflicted at birth, but you might consider the potential of the transit even if the Moon is well aspected. People survive this transit, but it helps if the parents are understanding and aware of it. If parents stop trying to hide the realities of life from the child, he can learn how to protect himself.

Young and inexperienced women living in cities become prey to rather unattractive men, or the kind of life that may include the misuse of drugs or alcohol. Under the Pluto-Moon transit, a sense of intuition is also highly developed, and this young person may be able to intuitively protect herself because she listens to her instincts. It is not uncommon for an immature and unaware female to be raped or sexually abused on this transit. These sexual experiences are seldom reported, for often these women feel that they brought on the experience. This is the rape that takes place because we trusted someone we knew. I've talked to many young women in the New York area who don't understand how they brought this kind of violence upon themselves, but they think they did. And they are not only afraid to report the crime, but they may never discuss the experience.

Five young women that I know had all been raped at some point by the same man! These were all middle class young women who had been trained to trust and respect older people. A forty year old type in the community had befriended them, originally meeting them in the local supermarket or on the street. He was jovial, and friendly, and kind, and married. He treated them all like an older brother would, meeting their dates and talking to them about how to live safely in New York City. These girls all had roommates and the man would drop over unannounced to visit on a Saturday or Sunday afternoon. At some point, he caught each of the girls home alone—and raped each one. Because she had let him into the apartment, she was afraid to tell her roommates about what had happened, so none of the roommates confided in each other, and the man still came by to visit. Finally, one of the girls felt so bad about what had happened, she sought solace from one of the girlfriends. She learned that he had raped them all. He knew they would be too embarrased to go to the police. And this is not an uncommon occurrence. It happpens to innocent women all too frequently. How do we astrologers counsel this problem? Most of us are afraid to admit that it exists. Or we see only gloom and doom with every transit. Somewhere there has to be a middle ground.

The Pluto transit brings an intensity to the body, a physical intensity or a vibration that can be recognized by those who prey on that intensity. Sometimes the transit can represent a fear of the intensity of life. The abyss that is represented in mythology is a part of the Pluto-Moon transit, for it represents an inner part of the self that needs to be investigated as a part of the gaining consciousness process. Most of the literature available concerns the young male hero off to find himself. He crosses the abyss, or he enters the abyss to struggle for his feeling identity.

The woman seeking identity is often pictured as a part of the abyss. She may be pictured as the waiting damsel in distress, looking for some prince to come along and save her from her plight. To some degree this is true as a young woman often looks to an animus type figure to come out of the subconscious and bring consciousness to her. But as a woman gets older and still seeks herself the literature seems to be buried or nonexistant. The ancient druid cults, the covens of ancient witchcraft have held onto the documents describing these inner processes, but they are mostly unavailable to the modern woman. How does a forty year old woman learn about her identity crisis as Pluto approaches her Moon by transit?

When Pluto transits the Moon, we have a chance to re-define what our emotions are all about. For a woman, it is a chance to add to her feminine role, to understand it at deeper levels. She can be saved by her knight, she can play damsel in distress, she can play mother and lover and she will eventually become free enough to be all those and a woman too. A woman can stand on her own. She can be both feminine, soft, nurturing and evolved enough to know the difference between conscious and unconscious loving. *Women's Mysteries,* by M. Esther Harding, may provide a source for the understanding of some of the changes that take place as a woman begins to discover her identity.

For a man, the Pluto transit to his Moon involves a different kind of change, for he now has a chance to learn how to experience the depth of his feeling nature. Because a man is often taught that it is not masculine to feel or to respond to his feelings, or to respond to any development of intuitive powers, he may try to close himself off under this transit, to protect himself from having to undergo these changes that may be so necessary to his development as a complete person. He must at some point in his life, get in touch with his feelings, his idea of feeling and nurturing. He must free himself from the feeling bonds that he has with his mother and teach himself how to use his emotional nature in a manner all his own. Most men never really break away from the mother, for they are often too frightened to approach the deep feeling changes within them, fearing that it may have something to do with the ties of early childhood. . . . or that it may bind him to his mother forever. As each of us learns to cope with our primal urges in order to bring them to consciousness, so must the man undergoing this kind of transit. It isn't easy for either sex for both are so immersed in cultural roles, we fear the exploration of the depths of consciousness.

The transit will affect our lives on many levels. Because Pluto symbolizes the underworld as well as the transformative process in a more constructive sense, the Pluto transit can indicate emotional upsets that take place as we are unseated by underworld events, or events promoted by the psyche. This can mean that our emotions become unfamiliar; we can be caught with our emotions on our face, like the proverbial egg. In order to avoid this kind of confusion, some people enter this transition period with many controls, hoping to keep a cover on the chaos within. The more we try to control our feelings, the more tense or intense we become. The Pluto transit signifies that we must let go of some of our controls, and learn to float in the universe. The letting go can be likened to learning how to float on water. If we relax, and let go, the water will hold us up and keep us afloat. If we can learn to approach this transit in a similar manner, the Pluto transformation will buoy us up and at the same time allow us to understand the powerful depths of human emotion.

• *Pluto-Mercury Transits*

Mercury symbolizes the five sense in the personality. We are especially concerned with the Mercury function as it describes the activity of the conscious mind. When Pluto comes along by transit to conjunct, square or oppose Mercury, the mental functions begin to change or transform. When Pluto trines or sextiles the natal Mercury, the thinking function operates on a highly creative level.

When the hard aspects transit Mercury, the mind function may be off balance for a while, unsure of itself. Thought patterns may be unfamiliar. Depending on the house placement and sign, the thought patterns can become intense, bringing certain periods of creativity if the energy is used constructively.

My clients don't complain about the creativity level during this transit. They talk carefully about feelings of stress. They voice concern over mental unbalance and wonder if a therapist is necessary. They fear the depth of the abyss. They may not put their fears in these words, but there seems to be some concern as to how long this period will last.

The artist doesn't complain, for most often the artist and writer is working diligently during this transit. The person in trouble is one who has talent but never thought to use it. It doesn't matter whether or not you publish a book under this transit but it matters that you write it. Poetry, pottery, novels, short stories, painting, the pursuit of any new intellectual interest—all these kinds of activities change the emphasis of the Pluto energy. We don't know where the energy will take us—it may just be an event in our lives or it may be the start of a whole new career or life interest.

The hard aspects sometimes indicate an insecurity about communication thereby creating a need to be in control of all communication. This can indicate a person who speaks very carefully, or one who delights in telling others what to think! One client, a copy editor, just loved hacking up manuscripts on this transit. She couldn't understand why her company didn't appreciate what she was doing. Essentially she was rewriting other people's work for the sheer joy of controlling it. Obviously, that is not the way to best use the transit. She could have, however used that energy to collaborate on a rewrite job— that would have put the energy to constructive use.

The need to control the mind, or to maintain control over the five senses can be quite a tense experience. Better to use the energy in some outgoing manner—do a bad painting, make an amateur clay pot. You might learn how to do it really well!

• Pluto-Venus Transits

This is usually a frustrating transit for when Pluto conjuncts, squares or opposes natal Venus it forces us to change our wants. Pluto transits are lovely because the "force" is not visible. It's somewhat akin to the force of the ocean—it just lays there looking innocent. And if we don't learn how to swim or float, the ocean can kill us; but if we learn its laws and its rules, it can be a valuable friend. Pluto hits Venus and says you must change. Natal Venus indicates the intellectual concept of what love is, and that concept is developed as a reaction to some ideas the mother had when the child was forming a personality. Her ideas of love will be shown by the sign Venus is in. Her problems relating to her femininity will be indicated by the natal aspects to Venus. Pluto comes along and says, "Get off this trip—change it. Don't depend on your mother's ways." And do we do it? Nope.

What do we appreciate—what kind of art, music, entertainment, home decor, clothing, or personal love do we want? And how are we to get what we want? From someone else? Nope. Pluto inspires us to go to others looking for a direction. We say we only want to know where we stand, so we cajole and push our lovers into telling us what their intentions are, when it really is a personal internal decision and not up to the lover at all. If you don't know what you want, this will not be a time when you can get centered because of a reaction from others. But we try.

Love is not giving and nurturing something or someone who kicks you. It is knowing what you want to give, and giving it with some kind of consciousness. Loving someone who can't give you the right time of day is a masochistic trip.

Pluto also symbolizes a desire for control and a manipulation of circumstances. It has something to do with obsession and under this transit we can try valiantly to control, manipulate or obsess over the people we think we love. And all our efforts are usually to no avail. If you didn't know anyone to love, what would you be doing? If this person you love wants out, if this person you love wants no part of you, what will you do? That will provide the answer you need. Make up your own mind as to what you want and then do it, says Pluto. We can't make anyone love us.

People who become obsessed with a lover or a potential lover will never win during this transit. You may be unconsciously looking for security, all the while you are calling it love. The other person may sense that you are looking for something that isn't really healthy and they run from you. You may be functioning from an unconscious need to manipulate or force others to bend to your will, to be open to your molding them. Yet you may be completely forgetting about what you need. Being loved on a volunteer basis is a far different thing than making someone love us.

And what shall we do with "winning?" It's very important to win on a Pluto transit to your Venus. This means you are okay—but it doesn't mean that at all. A deeply fulfilling love relationship cannot be built on your need to know where you stand. And what happens if the other person accepts you? Does that mean that you start laying down rules and regulations as to how he or she shall behave? And if you win, do you really want this person as a partner? Sometimes you win by losing. That becomes especially clear when you realize that in winning at the game of love under a Pluto transit, you may have just won a loser.

This transit can also signify some minor infection that you may have difficulty getting rid of. Some minor skin irritation that won't go away. It's best to take it to a doctor and get some help. The dumb infection I got was one that affected my pierced ears, which had been pierced years ago. I did not stop reinfecting until the transit went off. Other people have had skin infections, pimples and other silly infections that basically center around looking or feeling attractive and lovable.

One more thing should be mentioned about a Pluto-Venus transit, and that is the possibility of being attracted to someone who has an unsavory past. This can indicate a time when we are drawn to people who don't have a legal means of making a living, or people whose close associations are not always savory. Before commiting yourself to a relationship that will bother your sense of ethics later, give yourself a chance to determine whether or not you approve of this person's lifestyle. The transit does not guarantee that you will become involved with a gangster type, but the potential is there. Being aware of this possibility may save you pain later.

This transit really has to be interpreted according to the age of the individual living through it. Young people may have more difficulty with it than those who are older. The young folks need the words of caution for they are more open or receptive to the lower aspects of the transit. A person in the mid-thirties will respond differently when he understands that this transit gives him a chance to uproot himself from the old desire patterns. This is the transit that formulates the beginning of a whole new approach to love and the potential of a love relationship. This is the transit that will mark the point in time when a new personality emerges from an old one. The taste in music goes from rock to the classics, the conception of a good time changes from a loud party to a pleasant dinner in a nice restaurant. The ability to appreciate new things on many levels of the life experience start to emerge now. For this reason, the transit is worth the pain and the struggle.

• *Pluto-Mars Transits*

This transit combines the forces of the unconscious, the need for manipulation or control or obsession with the action principle. It also involves our sex drive. People react to this transit very differently. Some have to learn about anger, for the Pluto transit combines the anger of Pluto with the anger that is potentially tied to Mars. Some people become obsessive, some become preoccupied with sex, some become preoccupied with accomplishing some career goal.

The transit becomes more complex when Mars is also carrying other natal aspects, for they have to be worked with at the same time. This working process doesn't mean that we will permanently and forever work with this aspect, but that we now have a chance to work free of some of the more unconscious aspects of our personality. Some people respond to the Pluto-Mars transit by climbing into a shell and suppressing all the anger they feel. These are the more idealistic types who feel uncomfortable at feeling such intensity. They don't know what will happen, so they retire to their closet for a couple of years. It's really not too good to internalize the energy because we end up paying a high price for it—and the price relates to inner tension.

The person who uses this energy for work may accomplish great things, because he is driven by the action principle. This is the person who puts his head down and in two years time has moved from one end of the financial spectrum to the other.

Sexually this can be a trying transit, for it sparks the sex drive, and brings an intensity to it that may not be consciously realized. It means that we can draw unsavory types, or we can draw people who have violence and/or larceny in their hearts. This doesn't mean that you can't date, but that you should not take excessive risks during this period. The whole point of being forewarned about a transit is to alter your response to life to include the potential of the transit you are under. So you go to parties, for example, but you don't jump into a stranger's car to get a ride home. This is not the best transit for picking up strangers in bars either. If you blow the transit out of proportion, and become so frightened that you avoid all life experience, then astrological timing isn't really worth much. The overall guide to this kind of a transit is the awareness that this is not the best time for excessive risk taking.

If you are involved in a relationship already, this transit may be most inspiring sexually! You may find your sex drive is increased, you may be more stimulated than usual, you may want to transform your sexual energy and lift it to include a spiritual transformation. I'm not talking about celibacy but about adding another dimension to the sharing of your body and soul with another. Relationships formed during this transit may be sexually intense. If sex is the only basis for the relationship, you may want to wait until the transit is over before becoming permanently entangled. When the energy moves away, the sex drive will return to normal with only vestiges of the intensity remaining. And when the transit moves off, you also may need to have other aspects of a relationship fulfilled—you may decide that great sex isn't enough to compensate for a lack in other departments of life.

• *Pluto–Jupiter Transits*

Jupiter indicates how you relate. Its sign and position in the natal chart indicates where you most emphasize the relating principle. When Pluto comes along to transit Jupiter, the natal aspects to Jupiter will be activated as well as the transiting effect. And the additional natal aspects to Jupiter will make the transit more complex.

If you are accustomed to relating a certain way, Pluto can help you transform your relationship concepts. If you are not functioning on the most evolved level, you may become obsessive about relationships. You may want to manipulate people by not allowing them any spontaneity, by overplanning, etc. Or you may try to buy people causing them to be forever grateful because gobs of money have been spent on them when it really wasn't warranted. Or we may control others by keeping them so busy that they never have a chance to refuse us—we may plan to take them to dinner, to parties, to the theatre. Because we include them in so many of our plans, they never have a chance to ask us to do anything.

This is a period when we can develop new insights into what the relating process is so we can develop accordingly. We may blindly pursue a relationship even though we don't really understand why we are there. We may discover that sharing is a part of the relating principle, and we may begin to give differently, as well as expect different kinds of behavior to be directed at us. We may open up to completely different kinds of ideas—like the person who suddenly decides to take EST for example. It's a revolution in the relating principle.

Each person will respond to the transit differently. The differences will be symbolized by the sign Jupiter is in, and the natal aspects to it. The level of consciousness is also at play here, for the more self-responsible types will get more out of this transit than will those who aren't.

• *Pluto-Saturn Transits*

The hard aspects that occur between natal Saturn and transiting Pluto also cause a change in consciousness. Saturn symbolizes what we regard with caution, our feelings of restriction or fear, the psychological impact of our father on the early forming images that we carry in the subconscious.

Pluto can bring relief or release to the restrictive Saturnian facet of ourselves. Crystallization is a part of Saturn, and the Pluto energy keeps us from crystallizing that which we no longer need. It is the depth and breadth that force us to open up in some osmotic manner we haven't done before.

The transit becomes more complex and meaningful when natal Saturn aspects the personal planets. As Pluto requires us to understand the matters of life governed by the house it is transiting, we become more receptive as far as the Saturn house is concerned. If Saturn indicates what we have been afraid to explore because of programming we got when we were little, then the Pluto transit will help us open up.

This can be a chance to let go of old fears and cautions. Some people don't react to letting go very well, and the Pluto transit can indicate a period when they are really frightened of this new opportunity. We are afraid to face ourselves only as long as we believe we don't have the right to explore our own consciousness. We are afraid as long as we think there is nothing of beauty in us underneath the surface. These are the people who have really fallen for the cultural programming. We don't need to do that. We are free to make our lives what we wish, but we can't do that unless we know that we can.

The Saturnian programming that causes us to become cautious adults can be transformed. We don't throw caution to the winds, but we can get rid of some of the unnecessary caution, or feelings of worthlessness, and build upon our new found knowledge.

If natal Saturn symbolizes the affect of the father on the developing psyche, this transit can be important. If natal Saturn is afflicted, the hard aspects can tell something about what impact the father had. He may not have been aware of how he affected his child. For example, the child with Saturn square Mercury in the natal chart may have responded with too much fear when the father was around. The child may have been so afraid of the father, or may have been so chastised by the father, that communication with any authority figure became abnormally difficult. We don't know what would cause a child's reaction, we only know that a reaction occurred. If this is the case, the subsequent experience of this child may have developed a personality trait. This particular aspect, the Mercury square Saturn, causes words to come out with difficulty. These people sound harsh to others. They have difficulty communicating easily to those in authority—ranging from teachers in school to employers or any kind of an authority figure later in life. Others may think this person is hard, but the person who owns the aspect had difficulty expressing himself, and may have difficulty getting the words out. Because no one listened when he was younger, the subject has to be handled too quickly. This person tries to waste as few words as possible, trying to get his thought out before he is criticized or turned off. These kinds of natal aspects can be worked on during a Pluto transit because the owner of the aspect may become conscious of where his apprehensions and fears come from. These in depth awarenesses are hard to share with someone who doesn't understand. They are not easy conclusions to come to, either. The person undergoing a transformation during the hard aspect of a Pluto transit to Saturn will have to be somewhat self-aware in order to really benefit from the experience.

• *Pluto-Neptune transits*

This is not a particularly difficult transit even when Pluto is involved in a hard aspect to Neptune. Clients don't beat down your door to see you because of a Pluto transit hitting natal Neptune. They may if Neptune is aspecting some of the personal planets in the natal chart. The reason they come to see you is because of the affect of Pluto on the personal planet.

Neptune symbolizes the dreams of our generation. It symbolizes our lofty goals and wonderful spiritual inspirations. It symbolizes how we can delude ourselves, the kind of dream/delusion we are prone to, the department of life that we kid ourselves about. Our fantasy will be projected onto the life affairs described by the house Neptune is in. A Pluto transit through a house indicates a need to thoroughly understand the facets of life ruled by that house. So along with becoming aware of fifth house matters, for example, if Neptune is there natally, the transit of Pluto conjuncting natal Neptune will remove some of the veil of delusion caused by Neptune being there in the first place.

When the transit is a square or an opposition, the unveiling may not be that pleasant. If we don't learn easily, if we respond to the transit with the baser qualities of Pluto—like control stuff—perhaps we will be jolted out of our complacency.

The key to interpreting the transit is that dreams or fantasies or delusions about something must be transformed. Perhaps the transformation merely means bringing that facet of life into consciousness. That's a pretty big job in itself.

Because the transit is there for so long, because years are involved when using a ten degree applying orb for this transit, if one keeps an eye on the transit and uses a modicum of insight, it can be handled well before the transit becomes challanging.

This transit becomes more complex when involving the personal planets as well. They make the Pluto transit more imperative to handle consciously. The personal planets require attention from Pluto, and it may be more difficult to see the Neptunian dream.

• *Pluto-Uranus transits*

Uranus symbolizes the behavior pattern of a generation. It is not a personal planet, but rather symbolizes how a seven year segment of the population will behave. It symbolizes eccentricities, wilfullness, hardheadedness, and if Uranus carries hard aspects to the personal planets natally, then the transit becomes seriously significant.

In order to handle this transit period, it might be easier to look to the personal planets connected to the natal Uranus. Then the key to the transformation will emerge. Understanding and transformation are the keywords.

Because Uranus symbolizes independence and perhaps a facet of the individuation process, the transit can indicate a period of years when you are interested in bringing this process about in a more active manner. This may indicate a period where one pursues various philosophical interests, an interest in meditation, an interest in the occult or metaphysics, as long as these interests lead one down the road to better self-understanding.

Hard aspects involving Uranus in the natal chart usually indicate an abruptness relating to the department of personality symbolized by the personal planet. When we have a Venus-Uranus square natally, for example, we have a tendency to be somewhat abrupt about the things we like and those we love. We may begin and end relationships suddenly, we may not share our feelings about a relationship with the other person involved in it. While Pluto is transiting the natal square, we may begin to feel how we respond; we may begin to realize that we are imitating a parental pattern. Because we can become aware of a natal aspect, we can transform that energy into something constructive under a Pluto transit.

• *Pluto-Pluto transits*

When transiting Pluto forms a hard aspect to itself, we are not really experiencing a transit, but a part of a life cycle. This will be discussed in another volume.

• *Pluto transiting the Angles*

A Pluto transit to any of the angles will be one that you remember for a long time. Some of us might rather forget them, for they are not easy experiences. If you use a ten degree applying orb to any of the angles, Pluto will not present a problem. This gives you roughly five years to consider what the changes will be all about, what they might possibly encompass based on your chart. People involved in the process of true self awareness will gain immeasurably from these kinds of significant life changes.

First House. Pluto is coming out of the twelfth house as it begins to aspect the first house cusp. The transit signifies that we are in the process of pulling something out of unconsciousness (the twelfth) and bringing it into conscious awareness. The transit becomes very important when there are planets in the twelfth, because those planets symbolize aspects of personality that might not be as conscious as they should be. In the overall scheme of universal law, ignorance of the law is no excuse—so if we don't want to pay the penalty, we should be making some attempt to understand those aspects of ourselves. The transit indicates a kind of rebirth. As the Ascendant represents our new beginnings, our best foot forward in life, this transit symbolizes that we shall revolutionize or completely transform how we begin our day, how we begin new projects, how we present ourselves to others. Because the Ascendant represents the persona, some change will take place here, too.

Many astrologers don't understand that a major Pluto transit can be either internalized or externalized. Those people who are working with the energy from an internal point will be difficult to observe, as well as being difficult to counsel. The astrologer who projects fear and apprehension, or who counsels death and destruction to this kind of client will end up looking foolish. I've seen people go through serious internal crises, and the crises may affect both the business life and the personal life. Relationships have changed drastically. The career interest has changed.

We are suppose to change on this transit. Pluto says "Strip yourself of all that is unnecessary." If we are working in a particular career, better get prepared to change. If work habits have become habits, if we expect certain things to happen merely because we have put in our time, watch out! This transit requires that we change our approach to business—we can no longer look for the same benefits that used to occur twenty years ago; we can no longer handle situations the way we used to.

The Pluto transit is insidious—it's hard to see. It feels obscure. All we know is that we keep working and we aren't getting anywhere. We may *almost* get somewhere, but we just can't make it. It reminds me of a country analogy. Have you ever been driving on a slippery icy road? Try making it up a hill when the road hasn't been sanded or salted. You make a run at the bottom and spin your way to the top trying to avoid the ditches; and you almost make it. The car hangs there for an instant while you try vainly to coax it over the top. But you know you won't make it, and you'll have to back down the hill and try again. That's a Pluto transit over the ascendant—it keeps you working, but the results are just above the crest of the hill and you can't make it.

People who are completely unaware of a Pluto transit over the Ascendant may be prone to more obvious effects as the transit nears the exact conjunction. Young people have experienced physical violence. We can become involved in accidents and near death experiences as well as actually dying. But the people who suffer these consequences usually don't understand that they are under Pluto pressure. When they begin to feel out of control, when they feel they aren't getting anywhere, or when they are totally overcome with rage and anger, they draw the violent situation to them. This doesn't have to be the case. These are examples of the externalized transit.

In the internal process, the way to avoid pain is to keep questioning yourself. What needs to transform? What needs to change? What needs to be gotten rid of? As far as work is concerned, what are you learning that's new? How much complaining are you doing? Are those complaints centered around "the good old days?" If so, maybe the good old days have to go. If you are angry and resentful about the career you have chosen, why are you there? Complainers don't make it. How are the successful people in the business making it? Well? Please don't answer that all successful people are either crooks or cheaters, or the like. *You* have to change.

As far as the personal life is concerned, people and situations that are no longer needed will be removed. People die, lovers leave, old patterns are broken. It's a part of the freeing process. We humans are not too enthusiastic about change—we mourn it. The end of a relationship is a mournful time. We feel guilt and sorrow whenever we are transformed into an unfamiliar situation.

Young people need more counselling than older ones do. They need help understanding that it is not abnormal to leave home when you grow up. They need to learn that the natural stages of life are not abnormal and the counsellor can help them through these crises. Older people need a perspective. No one needs fear counselling. The rebirth of a life style lifts us so we can use the higher side of the sign ruling the Ascendant. In order to get to those qualities, we can't major in unconstructive anger reactions, or thoughtless beginnings. We need to plan our goals.

Fourth House. When Pluto moves toward the fourth house, we have five years to transform our attitudes about our home. This transformation includes freeing oneself from the effects of the early childhood environment, and changing the life expectany to something more constructive as far as what you wish to build in your life. We cannot create a comfortable home of our own if we are still tied to the early childhood experience. This experience may not be conscious but may be disclosed through slight intuitions and feelings that need to be brought into perspective on some useful level. Those who have been unable to build solid relationships by the age of thirty-five, may find that this transit helps free them of a past they never really thought about. Old relationships help the diagnosis.

The fourth house represents the foundation that is a part of heredity, the inherited past, and the past that forms the basis for this life. The Pluto transit symbolizes a time of change. The cocoon bursts, and we are free to let go of some of the inherited stuff, or keep it as we wish. Personally, I think it's a time to clean the house, physically, mentally and spiritually.

Some people will experience some mundane side effects during this transit, and the effect may be present the entire time that Pluto transits the fourth house. It signifies problems with the plumbing, with water, with sewage and all those unattractive things associated with Pluto. If that is the case, be happy it's the pipes in the house and not your own!

Seventh House. When Pluto spends a five year period coming to the cusp of the seventh house, you have a chance to prepare yourself for a transformation involving partnerships. Pluto is coming through the sixth house, which symbolizes how we handle our daily grind or the day-to-day responsibilities. Those day-to-day things also involve how we treat our partners, both business and marriage. We are beginning a new phase in life, we are lifting the possibility of our relationships to another level. This may involve the ending of a relationship that is no longer needed, or the beginning of a whole new attitude about relationship potential.

The most difficult part of this transit is the changing relationship needs. We tend to view our partners as a part of our foundation. They become rather like our parents were when we were children—they are there when we need them. That is not always the case in real life, and some people are really upset when they discover that they don't know the person they've been married to for the last ten years. Relationships should be constantly changing as the partners change. But they don't. We don't listen to each other. Sometimes we resent the person we live with becoming involved with something new. The partner picks up on the negative vibration and stops sharing. The Pluto transit will change all this. The changes will take place either easily because we learn to open up and share or the hard way, because a relationship ends. The transit is so slow, it takes so long to make the exact conjunction to the seventh house cusp, that we have plenty of time to notice the signals on the way to change.

This transit can completely transform the concept of relationships. However, while it is happening, Pluto will also be opposing the Ascendant. This transit tends to make people feel as though they have no control over the events in the life. It can seem as though the partner is coercive, or that personal freedom, or the freedom to do what you want to do regarding career is being hampered by the partner. The transit signifies a change in the attitude about cooperation. This change will probably affect all four angles in the chart to some extent. And out of the frustration comes the change.

Tenth House. When Pluto moves into a ten degree orb of the tenth house cusp, it begins to effect the public image, the honors that we strive for, the recognition of the career goals. This signifies a five year building period that concerns changes in career goals. This would be a time to work toward making those changes so that the maximum energy can be gained from the transit.

This would be a time to move carefully regarding the career, though. It is not the time for short cuts, graft or underhanded dealings. When Pluto culminates at the tenth house cusp, the chickens can come home to roost, and the chances for being discovered with egg on your face are better than at other times in life. So moves should be made that are based on an honest desire to move ahead. Again, the universe doesn't hurt you if you haven't brought it on yourself, so any honest endeavor shouldn't be avoided.

Another underhanded side of a Pluto transit may indicate a period where you attract people from the underworld. This doesn't just mean that some young lady dates a dope-seller; it can mean that legitimate business people may be confronted by those people who wish to buy their way into a "clean" business to wash some dirty money. When people offer you too good a deal during this period, you may want to be extra careful and check it out.

Whenever a transiting planet conjuncts an angle in the chart, pressure is put on at least two major life areas. If the Ascendant is affected, there will also be an opposition involving the seventh house. If the four major angles are in a square aspect to each other, any transit to the angles will become most important, for those four areas are up for change. These changes shouldn't be feared, because the Cardinal cross in the natural zodiac symbolizes change. Change is not abnormal. It's always happening.

Part 2
Individual
Case Studies

Diagnosis

When I first began to work with transits, I would pencil them into the natal chart. Whenever someone made an appointment for a reading I would use the transit positions of the day scheduled for the reading. Then I made a list of the planets in the natal chart, and next to the list would go the time periods of a transit's effect. Before the client came in for the appointment, the transits and possible transits for the next year had already been worked out. This doesn't take long. After one gets some practice at doing it, the calculations for the transits can be worked out in about fifteen minutes.

The major problem in reading transits is that of synthesis. Two things are being combined, for we are going to talk about what the transit is doing to the natal chart at the same time that we discuss how the transit is setting off the natal chart. Usually more than one major transit is hitting simultaneously, so the issue becomes more complicated. Astrology students are sometimes prone to "proving how much they know" and sometimes forgetting that the client has a personality. Sometimes the astrology student is so interested in predicting correctly, that the student forgets to listen to his client. Sometimes we give more information than the client is willing to hear, and we usually do this because we are trying too hard to be helpful. We want to share everything we know even if it kills the client!

When people want a reading they are in some kind of a crisis period. And here the astrologer is coping with two factors. Some clients don't want to tell you what the problem is because they can't voice it; they're afraid to talk about it; they haven't been able to name it yet; or they think you are some kind of a mystical psychic fortune teller and they want you to guess what the problem is. I won't let clients put words into my mouth. Some of them are looking for an astrologer, a fortune teller, a counsellor who will solve their problems for them. They want you to make their decisions. However, since you are not going to be around to see how they handle the day-to-day problems, you have no control over the outcome of an event. If you make a decision for your client, that client can blame you for making a wrong decision for him. So it's wiser to stay out of that.

When reading transits, you also don't know whether or not your client has begun to be self-responsible. If you do a natal reading first, the conversation you have regarding the natal aspects, and the client's response to your descriptions should give you some insight into how he is responding to life's vicissitudes. The transits cannot bring any more into the life than the owner of that life is willing to take responsibility for. For example, we all can learn a great deal from our Saturn transits, but if a client chooses to see the Saturn transit in a negative sense, there is little you can do to "make" him understand the more constructive energy symbolized by the transit.

You may run into a client who has little self insight, who has little self-perspective and little feeling of self-responsibility. This person may also be an extroverted type, and by extrovert I mean a person who looks outside of himself in order to ascertain his worth. This kind of a person is crushed when he loses a job, for example, for his title meant that he was worth something; without it he is nobody. When reading for these kinds of people, we must be cautious, for we don't want to talk to someone about too much in one session, as the personality may not be able to accept all the information.

Please don't confuse a client's ability to respond to information with his educational background. People who don't have a college degree are just as realistic, and perhaps more so, than people who are thought to be well-educated. Poor people have usually lived closer to reality in their effort to survive than those who have been protected from Mother Nature because of money. You may approach each client differently. You may talk about different things with a person who has more education. You can talk about Jungian archetypes with someone who is familiar with them, while those words won't be understood by a construction worker who has never read Jung. But you can get the same information across to him if you learn how to do it—if you can reach into his head to find some way to communicate with him. And last but not least, you cannot judge your client by the way he or she looks.

Sometimes clients play with you; sometimes they hide themselves in an effort to see what you know and how judgemental you are.

Even though you have prepared yourself to talk to a client about a year's worth of transits, you may never have a chance to do it. We're going to work with some case studies to show you how to track the transits, and how transits tie into the natal chart. But in a real session, you may never get to all this material. On the one hand your client may not be developed enough to handle it. On the other, he may be in such a crisis period that the session will be devoted to helping him understand that particular crisis. Beginning students often become frustrated because they haven't been able to "read" the chart. But the whole point of getting into this kind of astrology is to help someone develop a clearer perspective of who he is, and that may not require a thorough reading of the chart!

This field in astrology is essentially a new one. Astrologers have been considered fortune tellers. Astrologers used to specialize in horary astrology—the timing of a question. These questions rarely had anything to do with the process of individuation, they had more to do with "Will I win my court case?" or, "Will I get married?" We are now trying to use the symbolism to counsel people as they grow. We can use the symbolism to help others better understand themselves. And this means that we have to be astute enough to recognize when enough is enough. We have to learn how to read body language; we have to learn about people's defenses and what they mean; we have to learn something about basic psychological counselling procedures so that we don't hurt our clients more than we help them. The keyword to learning this process is "slow" for when we aren't sure of what we are doing, nothing is better than something.

I recommend that students participate in workshops that feature working with natal charts of people they know well. Several astrologers have begun to teach these kinds of workshops, so that students can learn how to counsel. We have wonderful information at our disposal but when we misuse it, we become like children trying to drive a car on a speedway when we've never been behind a wheel before. We, too, have to assume responsibility for what we do. My way of handling clients is with a prayer, for I pray that I will say the right thing, and know when to stop talking. And my intention is to help that person, not judge him.

We learn how to read charts by practicing. One of the blessings of being a student is that the person who seeks you out for a reading in the beginning can only handle what you have to tell him. I look back on some of my first readings, wishing that I could share the knowledge that I have now with that person, but he didn't want it. If he had, he would have gone to someone else! And you learn from every reading you do. You'll learn how to talk to different types of people, you'll learn what people respond to best, you'll learn how to share your information in a palatable way. You'll see how aspects work, too, because as you talk to people, you'll find out that certain aspects don't work like you thought they would. Or you find out that some people use their aspects and others are used by them. You'll learn about the consciousness level of an individual. All your experience should help you to become more conscious, more aware of what is happening in the world around you— what goes on in the minds of humanity. Please don't get uptight, please stay open, please stay humble, please learn as much as you can. And learn the balance between a client who doesn't accept what you say, and the validity of the aspects!

When I first began to do readings, I read for friends. When I tried to talk to them about aspects in the natal chart, or about transits that affected the personal life, they denied what I said. I got little positive feedback. However, when I began to read for strangers, people who didn't know me personally, the feedback was totally different. The client really appreciated what I said, and the client wasn't defensive of his position. I began to realize that this work was too personal for me to do with my friends. However, you can learn a lot from watching your friends!

Even when you have a paying client, you may run into a person who won't accept what you have to say. If this happens, it may be better to let it slide. In some cases, I've offered to read for nothing, or I've offered to stop the reading because there was no point in going further. Those clients have always paid me after the reading.

You may find the problem with the client is based on words. You said something that the client can't accept because you have different definitions. If you wait long enough, the client will start talking the aspect and you can bring it up again. I tried to talk to one client about her resentment toward her mother, and she denied that she felt that way. An hour later, she got caught up in a story she was telling me about her mother, and the venom and the bitterness started coming out. I said, "Remember I tried to tell you about that? That's what I was talking about." Then you can begin to explain how the transit is working with the natal aspect, and how the client can work through it.

• Chart A

In order to see how transits work on a natal chart, we'll use the same two charts that were used to delineate the Mars transits. The Mars transits have indicated the physical energy available to these people, and you can see how they are working if you look back to pages 37 and 42.

Chart A is the chart of a young woman born in 1946. I have permission to use her chart as long as I don't reveal her name and her birth data, so it has not been provided. Her birth data came from a birth certificate, and the chart was processed by Astro-Computing Services.

The transits we'll discuss now are those associated with growth and change on an internal level. In your ephemeris, you'll see where the slower moving planets are located on January 1, 1980. They should be added in the appropriate places on the outside of the chart wheel, so you can keep them from becoming confused with the natal planets. See Chart A. It is not necessary to be so visual, but I find that the natal chart combined with the transits gives me a better picture during the reading. The transiting planets will always activate the aspects in the natal chart. So I draw in my natal aspects as well as the transits, so I can see the picture more clearly. Sometimes we can forget planets or natal aspects under the pressure of doing a reading, and the visualization of the chart helps keep a perspective.

The first thing you'll notice is that all the transiting heavy planets are sitting between the sixth and eighth houses. We don't use the transiting Sun, Moon, Mercury or Venus as these planets move too quickly. The slower moving planets signify internal changes. Because these transits are hitting one particular area of her chart, she will be concerned with matters symbolized by those houses for the next several years.

The transit emphasis concerns her work, her employee-employer relations, how to handle the responsibilities of the daily grind, which comes from the sixth house. The stress from Uranus in the seventh house indicates a change in both business and personal partnerships. Neptune in the eighth house emphasizes partner's finances, legal matters, IRS, taxes, inheritance or inherited responsibilities, her own process of transformation. Not all of these catagories will be active at the same time, and she may not be concerned with all the possible forms of transit expression, but this gives you, the reader, a bird's eye

CHART A

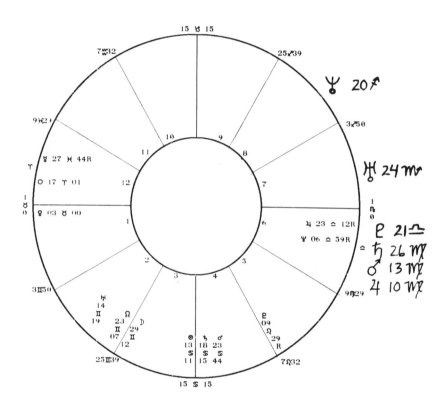

view of the probable stress areas or areas of change in her life that she may wish to discuss with you. When you talk to her, she'll tell you what they are, you don't have to guess the phase she's in.

I like to work with the transits of the slower moving planets first as they set the mood of the chart and indicate the less stressful energy. The energy is less stressful because it is in effect for a long time and it signifies the major transformations that she is in the process of making. Saturn and Jupiter move more quickly than do Uranus, Neptune and Pluto. Saturn and Jupiter will symbolize more of a crystallization process that will effect the changes made internally because of the energy coming from Uranus, Neptune and Pluto.

• *Pluto*

Pluto is at 21° Libra on January 1, 1980. By transit it's in her sixth house. Generally speaking, Pluto in the sixth indicates some major changes in attitude regarding health, work, how to handle the daily grind, as well as how to handle other employees. Because Pluto moves so slowly it will be in that house for years. This should tell you that the transformation process is a slow one, not one that she need to become panicy about, not one that she might miss like a Mars transit.

The planets in Cardinal signs that have been activated by the Pluto transit are:

Sun at 17° Aries
Saturn at 18° Cancer
Mars at 23° Cancer
Jupiter at 23° Libra

Because Pluto has passed the 17 and 18 degree mark of a Cardinal sign, the Sun and Saturn are no longer as actively involved in the transit as they once were. However, because Pluto is approaching 23° Libra (it is now at 21°) both Mars at 23° Cancer and Jupiter at 23° Libra are under pressure. Since all four planets are involved in a t-square (an opposition tied to two squares), the tension caused by the t-square will remain

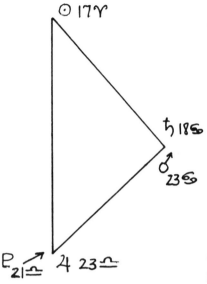

active until Pluto goes off the 23° mark. Looking ahead in your ephemeris, you'll see that Pluto hits 23° Libra on December 11, 1980. Don't believe what you see, though for as you move into 1981, you'll see that Pluto retrogrades back over the t-square again. On March 15, 1981, Pluto hits 23°44′ of Libra again, and it stays in orb until October 4, 1981. Does that end it? Yes, it does. Pluto will retrograde again, but it only goes back to 24° and we are interested in 23. Once the transiting aspect hits the exact degree of a conjunction, square or opposition, the pressure is off.

The Pluto transit to her Cardinal t-square places special emphasis on her Mars-Jupiter natal square. This natal aspect indicates that she will be learning something about taking action (Mars) under the influence of an over-expanded Jupiter in her lifetime. In other words, she may try to do too much, she may have periods where she doesn't give a damn, because the Jupiter square can express in an "I don't care" kind of way. This means she may have a tendency to become overly enthusiastic, overly productive, or overly involved in her work. She may also have moods where she is extremely demanding sexually, because Mars symbolizes the sex drive. Under the Pluto transit, the desire for sex may be increased.

Because Mars conjuncts Saturn natally, she may run hot and cold sexually. Because both Mars and Saturn square the Sun, she may periodically take action (Mars) against (square) her own best interests (Sun). In plain English, her choice of sexual partners may not always be people who will support the needs of her Sun. Or her sexual needs may cause some difficulty when she attempts to develop some other facet of personality. Or her need for a sexual-emotional relationship requires that she do so at the expense of other interests. And mixed in with it all, is a basic lack of trust in men in general, and authority figures especially (Saturn square the Sun). So she can run hot and cold.

My observation is that she has been working on this t-square, because she has learned how to work at the management level, which means that she must be cooperative with the people she works with. She cannot be a rebel, or obviously anti-authoritarian. The problems signified by the t-square may be that of over-working or that of picking men who are basically uncooperative or non-supportive of her needs as a woman. This may be an area of discussion when the reading takes place.

Pluto is concentrating energy at this t-square and during the period of years when it first went into Libra (around 1972) it began to focus energy on these personality development needs. The transit is not meant to hurt her, but to help her transform herself, to help her to become more aware of who she is. Her Sun at birth is besieged by hard aspects from Mars, Saturn and Jupiter. All these pressures can cause the poor little Sun to hide itself, to avoid pursuing its own goals while she is reacting to the pressure of Mars, Jupiter and Saturn. Pluto says it's time that this energy get into a better balance. The balancing energy comes from Libra.

In order for the process of individuation to take place, the transit must bring a chance for consciousness to develop. This is a period (of ten years—from 1972–1982) when a transformation of personality can occur. She is a relatively young woman, so in her 20's and 30's she is undergoing a transformation that affects her children, her love life, her career, her inner self. and the timing of the Pluto transit couldn't be better. These kinds of changes are more beneficial when we are young, for she is both old enough to understand what the changes are all about, and young enough to have time to apply and develop what she has learned.

Pluto hitting Mars at 23° Cancer (a square) says she must learn a new way to take action, she must now learn something more about her sexual needs, she needs to learn something about anger. Not that what she has done so far is bad, but that it needs to develop a broader perspective. Mars in Cancer expresses emotionally; it may take action as a little girl or a big momma, and the female balance called woman that lies between little girl and big momma will develop now. Pluto brings anger and control needs to the fore, and Mars can be angry under the pressure from Pluto, so action may be taken in anger, or she may become angry because of her intense sexual needs of the moment. Underneath the anger is creative energy and warmth, if she can figure out what causes the anger so she can get rid of it.

Pluto hitting Jupiter puts an accent on her ability to relate, how she reaches out. She has done this with difficulty in the past, for Jupiter opposes the natal Sun. She can transform her "reaching out" ability, so she can reach out at the same time that she includes her self (the Sun). Jupiter opposing the Sun relates to the needs of others while compromising her own. This can cause anger, bitterness and tension. But Pluto says the transformation is at hand if she wants it.

• *Neptune*

The next slowest moving planet is Neptune. By transit it is at 20° Sagittarius on January 1, 1980. It is transiting through her eighth house. Neptune brings delusion and illusion to the house it moves through. It shows us our blind areas so Neptune in the eighth would indicate that she would be more apt to be blind to things like partner's finances, the possibility of her own transformation, matters having to do with inheritance, taxes, money coming in from others. She might be overly susceptible to other people's ideas at this time as well, for she may see them through a cloud of idealism.

Neptune is symbolic of inspiration as well. She may be as inspired by these issues as she may be deluded. She may be a combination of both. The blindness to reason that is suggested by the Neptune transit is there for a reason. I feel it relates to our need to begin to trust our intuition. In eighth house matters, she could do well listening to her intuitive impressions and feelings.

Neptune is setting off her Nodal axis, so generally there will be opportunities for her to advance herself in some way as long as Neptune aspects the Nodes. Different astrologers view the Nodes of the Moon differently, and you may wish to pursue your personal interests as to what the Nodes symbolize. I feel that the North Node signifies opportunity and the South Node becomes important when we don't use our opportunities well. The Neptune transit will activate the Nodes until January 3, 1981.

Neptune by transit is opposing her natal Moon. The Moon squares Mercury at 27° Pisces, and is also squaring Neptune at 6° Libra in the natal chart. Some astrologers would say she has a t-square. Others won't accept the nine degree orb for an opposition between Mercury and Neptune. I do. If the t-square is accepted, the Neptune transit will keep the t-square alive until Neptune transits into 6° Carpicorn in 1987.

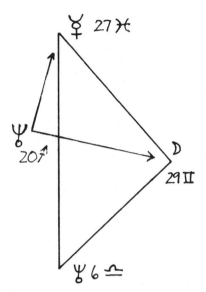

However, the main emphasis of the moment is the opposition of Neptune to her natal Moon at 29° Gemini. Using a ten degree applying orb, the transit will be active until December 28, 1983. This gives her plenty of time to learn how to cope with the Neptunian energy. If Neptune signifies delusion-illusion, the transit will spark some delusion about her emotional responses or some illusion regarding her feelings, or a combination of the two. This may mean that she isn't aware of what her true feelings are. Neptune can signify inspiration, so she may feel inspired or creative during this period. Because she is feeling inspired, her emotional reactions may be changing to a different perspective. Neptune can indicate impersonal or Platonic love. She may respond emotionally to new kinds of relating situations. She may adjust her sexual feelings during this period. She may broaden her perspective on love.

Neptune by transit devitalizes, so she may feel tired, she may have trouble sleeping, her vitality may be lowered. She may need more sleep than usual, she may feel more tired than usual, she may not be able to handle pressure as well due to her lack of energy. She may be so tired that she can no longer contend with emotional trauma that is unnecessary, or emotional trauma that is too draining of her energy. This results because of the Moon being involved. This may facilitate a change in her emotional response nature.

Because Neptune by transit is squaring natal Mercury she may develop new insights into learning how to express herself emotionally. The difficulty in self expression is caused by the natal square between Mercury and the Moon. When she was a child, her mother had difficulty expressing herself as a woman, or as a person. Now may be the time when the daughter, the woman in Chart A, learns how to talk more openly about her feelings.

The Neptune transit squaring Mercury also enhances the creative response, so writing, publishing and any creative endeavor can be inspirational during this period. Her psychic and intuitive abilities are more sensitive now. If you want to pursue the Neptunian influence in greater depth, I recommend the recently published *The Neptune Effect* by Patricia Morimando.

Although the aspect is considered out of orb at the moment, the natal Moon square Neptune will be affected by the Neptune transit as well. Between 1980 and 1987 she will be learning something about her notion of femininity, about what a woman is. In the natal chart, the Moon-Neptune square signifies the possibilitiy that her mother influenced her at a very young age in such a way that she has some strange ideas about what a woman is. Either her mother was lying about herself as a woman, presenting herslf as someone she wasn't, or she gave her child such an idealized version of the concept of woman that her daughter assumes she must be some kind of a Madonna. If that was the case, during the next several years, she will begin to work herself free of the image. She may stop trying so hard because she doesn't have the energy to work so hard to please those around her.

• *Uranus*

On January 1, 1980, Uranus is at 24° Scorpio. It is transiting her seventh house of marriage and partnerships. It has been there for several years. During the period of years that Uranus moves through her seventh, she will learn about who likes her and who doesn't (as the seventh also rules open enemies), and she can learn how to respond to those who don't like her. Her image is changing. Her ideas of marriage and partnership are changing.

Uranus brings with it an opportunity for self liberation from the confines or restrictions given us by our early childhood environment. Because Scorpio rules her seventh, she may have strong ideas about having to reform or change her partners. But someone who needs reforming isn't qualified to be a partner by definition. Maybe she'll learn that a woman's role is not limited to Emily Bronte's Jane Eyre. Scorpio indicates a natural desire to reform a partner when it rules the seventh. Add this to the natal Moon-Neptune square and she may have some preconceived notions about her role as a woman that include doing too much or trying too hard.

Uranus is not making any hard aspects to any planets in her chart, so its seventh house influence is a general one. Now we've looked at all the "heavies" and it's time to move on to the more personal and abrupt indications signified by Saturn and Jupiter.

• *Saturn*

On January 1, 1980, Saturn is at 26° Virgo. It's transiting the sixth house, requiring that she crystallize some ideas regarding health, work, service to others, handling fellow employees, her employer, even coping with the daily grind of running her home. Saturn transits indicate what you need to learn about, where you need to develop a more mature attitude considering what you've learned up to this point, how old you are, and where you are heading. Saturn brings in a realistic perspective as well as a crystallization of ideas that have been floating around for a while.

We discussed an out of sign t-square between natal Moon, Mercury and Neptune. The Saturn transit is giving her a chance to

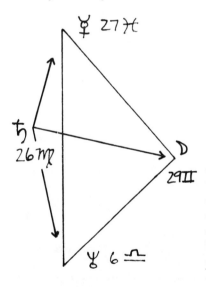

crystallize some of the Neptunian inspiration. Everywhere she turns in an immature manner, Saturn will block her path, standing as the Cosmic Cop that points the way to the future and bars any immature attempts to continue on as before. This is a serious emotional transit and a difficult one. She may be coping with stress and depression. The transit signifies a period that a psychiatrist would call a life crisis. I'm not suggesting that you send her to a therapist, or that she can't handle the crisis by herself, but rather that as an astrologer, *you* should understand that she is in a crisis and that crisis is okay. It's a natural phenomenon.

Let's consider the planets under stress one at a time. First of all, Mercury is at 27° Pisces Retrograde. Let's look back in the emphemeris to see when the stress began to build. Saturn hit 17°44' of Virgo on

September 9, 1979. She began to take her Mercury seriously at that point. She began to regard her words with caution, stopping to carefully evaluate and select the words that best suited her ideas. In the process of doing this, she began to change. She may not have even been conscious of it. She probably spoke harshly without meaning to. Those who knew her probably saw her as either hard or withdrawn. She didn't feel that way inside though, and there were probably verbal misunderstandings with co-workers and family members. Saturn causes concentration problems as well, so she may have some difficulty coping with noise and confusion; her memory may not be what it has been; she may have had problems using her five senses so minor ailments may crop up regarding eyes, ears, nose, etc.

Saturn hit 19° Virgo 12' on September 27, 1979 and began to square her Moon by transit. During the time it takes Saturn to move ten degrees (about a year) she will be regarding her body, her emotional needs, her response to her life style, family, friends, co-workers, work needs with great caution as the Moon rules the emotional response to these categories.

She may feel bitter and resentful that her emotional needs are not being satisfied. When Saturn transits in hard aspect to the Moon, the emotional needs, a need for affection and love (not sex love, but warmth) all come to the surface. They surface because you aren't getting what you need. Saturn teaches us about how we need to mature as well as what those needs are in the first place. People don't make large strides in the growth process because everything is going well— we usually discover what our emotional needs are when they are lacking. We discover that we don't want to accept second best any longer.

This is a time when she will re-evaluate what she thinks about the business of love and caring. She will make some mature judgements about what she needs emotionally now. Her new needs relate to how old she is and what she feels she needs to develop. You don't have to predict how she will change—it's better to help someone understand what the foundation of the transit is and then let him build his own reactions.

Saturn transiting the Moon says that she will be looking at relationships. If she lives with someone, she will look at the relationship seriously as she is diagnosing what she is getting out of it versus what she is putting into it. And if the balance doesn't come up close to fifty/fifty, she'll be resentful, and perhaps rightfully so. Because the transit is so powerful, she will discuss her feelings with her mate. This is a serious evaluation period in a relationship. If the partner is cooperative, the relationship makes it; if the partner has no understanding of the transit, the relationship may end. But when you read this chart, you don't know how the stress will be handled. Relationships should survive Saturn transits. But sometimes they don't.

The Saturn-Moon transit sometimes brings the loss of a loved one with it. Women in the life are usually involved in the loss. I think it has to do with learning about love that isn't sex love. In my experience, people have become estranged from female friends during this transit—a friend might move from New York to California, causing a feeling of loss because you miss the companionship. Some people have had an old or trusted friend turn on them giving no explanation of the incident. In some cases female relatives pass over, and this relative could be an aunt, a grandmother or a mother. However, the Saturn transit doesn't guarantee the death of a relative or the loss of a friend. It just indicates a possibility.

In counselling people about this transit, I mention the possibilities. If a female friend should move, this person will cope with the feeling of loss when we lose the comradeship we experience with a friend. If a friend turns on us, she can understand what the meaning behind the loss is about; if an older relative is not well, this would be a year to spend allowing time for visits to the family rather than avoiding family get-togethers.

During the time of a Saturn transit, she may find it necessary to develop new friends because the old ones aren't available when she needs them. This should not be a resentful period, but should be seen as a period when one enlarges the emotional scope in order to become less dependent. If we only have one friend, we become too dependent on sharing with that person. This is a period to open up to other people.

Saturn at 26° Virgo will go on to conjunct natal Neptune. This transit brings some grief with it, some depression and some feeling of hopelessness because good old Saturn, symbolizing Father Time and the Grim Reaper is crystallizing on her natal Neptune. Neptune in the natal chart symbolizes our dreams, our inspirations, our druthers, and Saturn by transit rips off the rose-colored glasses and says, "This is reality, kid." And we say, "Is that all there is?" And Peggy Lee sang it to all the folks going through a Saturn-Neptune transit. Saturn will force her to take a new look at career goals and dreams of the perfect relationship. She doesn't have to give up her ideals; she just needs to change her approach a bit.

At the same time, the natal square between the Moon and Neptune is being crystallized by Saturn, and she is being pressured to take a new look at her concept of womanhood. Saturn is hitting the Moon-Neptune square, Neptune by transit is hitting the Moon-Neptune square, and Uranus is transiting the seventh house. This indicates a fairly heavy dose of change regarding her role as a woman, a partner, a lover. She should have some very different ideas about herself as a woman in a relationship when these transits are over.

One of the basic feelings present in a Saturn transit is a feeling of restriction—of being blocked. The blocks can be used as sign posts along the road. The difficulty doesn't mean we should give up the quest, but that we have to reassess or redirect our energies to atttain the quest. And we need to drop the past, to let go of old restrictions in order that we become free to pursue the "new me." Saturn doesn't pull any punches; Saturn doesn't hit us over the head if we are reading the messages. We must change on this transit; we must crystallize the aspects of personality being touched by the transit; we must change. Saturn says you can feel anyway you want to, but your feelings must hold water. They must be real. Saturn cuts through the pie-in-the-sky stuff and says put your money where your mouth is. Saturn is not unkind. We sometimes think the energy is unkind, because we are not well-prepared for coping with reality. But reality can be beautiful.

The Saturn transit will be active until Saturn reaches 6° Libra. It will stay on her Mercury until September 3, 1980; it will be hitting the Moon until September 15, 1980. At that time she should feel a tremendous release as the pressure will be off those two personal planets. However, Neptune at 6° Libra in the natal chart will keep the Saturn transit alive until November 22, 1980. Saturn will retrograde in 1981, and on March 20, 1981 it comes back to natal Neptune. It will remain in orb until August 16, 1981. Many changes will be taking place during this period.

• *Jupiter*

On January 1, 1980 Jupiter is at 10° Virgo and it is beginning to transit her sixth house. This indicates even more emphasis on work, daily grind, health, working with others. It retrogrades (moves backward in the zodiac) out of her sixth and into the fifth on January 19, 1980. It stays in the fifth until July 21, 1980 so she'll have a period where she enjoys entertaining at home, being in love, dealing with her child. Because of the Saturn transit to her Moon, she may be doing some re-evaluating of what her entertainment needs are, what her love needs are, and how she wants to respond to her child. On July 22, 1980, Jupiter returns to the sixth, bringing sixth house matters back into focus.

Her natal Uranus is at 14° Gemini, so from January 1, 1980 until May 3, 1980, and again from June 20th until August 16, 1980, Jupiter will square natal Uranus by transit. Uranus sextiles the Sun natally, so this transit will activate opportunity for her to express herself. It may bring opportunity or promotion at work. There are no hard aspects to Uranus, so the square should not bring any problems. If it does, it may activate some kind of eccentricity or stubborness tied to her behavior pattern.

On August 30, 1980, Jupiter transits into a ten degree orb (17° Virgo 39') of her natal Mercury (27° Pisces 44'). It begins to activate the t-square involving Mercury, Moon and Neptune. Saturn is there already, so the tension mounts.

Jupiter opposing Mercury by transit indicates a tendency for hasty words that might be better curbed. The square to the Moon indicates a tendency to overrelate emotionally, and the upcoming conjunction to Neptune indicates an activation of the inspiration/delusion syndrome, suggesting she may be highly flammable during this period! The tension lasts until Jupiter reaches 6° Libra on December 7, 1980. So from August until December she'll be coping with a Jupiter transit.

I have found Jupiter a difficult transit because it has made me painfully aware of my more unattractive aspects natally, and I imagine it will do the same for her. She may have a chance to use the energy constructively by beginning to consciously *feel* the natal aspect working within her. The programming of a natal aspect is so engrained in our personality, that we sometimes don't even relate to having it. Jupiter will make her aware, and therein lies its value as a transit. It helps make us aware of what we are working with.

We've just discussed a lot of material, and the probability of being able to share all this information with a client is low. But as astrologers, all these transits, and all the possibilities of what a transit may signify should be available to you in case you need to use it. After typing up this list of transits, I showed my notes to my client and we discussed what I said.

Two things were very important to her. One was the Pluto transit, for she wanted to confirm some of her feelings about it. We needed to clarify language. She was aware of the transit going on in her life. The other transit that we discussed was that of Saturn to the natal Moon. All the things described were an issue. She needed to talk about her changing consciousness about her relationship, the changes in how she was feeling, the changes in what she considers her needs to be, the fact that those needs are not being satisfied, the fact that she can feel impending changes in her emotional expression. If we had had a session together, these would have been the two transits that would have been discussed during the session.

• *Chart B*

The transits to Chart B are completely different than the ones for Chart A. Although the planets are in the same place on January 1, 1980, the transits will affect this person in a very different manner. I purposely used two people born in Cardinal signs, so that you could see both the similarities of the Cardinal pressure and the differences in how it manifests for different people.

Chart B is of a young man. He is about thirty years old. His identity and birth data are withheld to protect his identity. The natal chart was based on data provided from his birth certificate, and the chart was processed by Astro Computing Services.

In the discussion of this chart, I want to bring up the possibilities for crisis solving as well as discussing the problems that may be affecting him during this time period. Not all the possibilities or potential in this chart will be activated, for each of us has free will and we each choose what direction we move in. The point of looking at all the possibilities is to better prepare us for any eventual conversation that may come up during the session. We cannot possibly discuss the material we discuss here in one session with a client. You would probably pick and choose what material you would spend time on. The client will also wish to center his session on personal conflicts that he feels need resolution.

• *Pluto*

On January 1, 1980, Pluto is at 21° Libra. By transit it is in the twelfth house. He has six Cardinal planets in his chart, but none of them are

CHART B

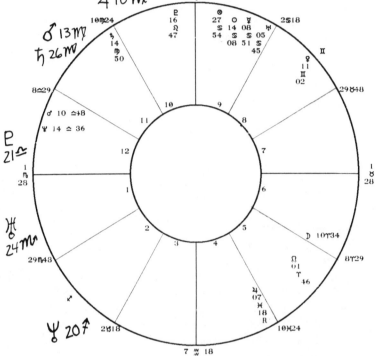

presently being affected by the Pluto transit because the highest degree in Cardinal signs is 14°. The twelfth house has been called the house of self-undoing, the house of unconscious matters; it is said to be a psychic and spiritual house. It also rules hidden enemies (or those people you don't recognize as not being your friends). Because Pluto is transiting through the twelfth, he probably is beginning to cope with thoughts that may have been buried in his subconscious. He is beginning to examine some of his ideas, his motives for doing what he does; perhaps he's beginning to look at personal issues that have not been thought about before.

Both natal Mars and Neptune are in the twelfth. Mars relates to his work, how he takes action, his sexuality. Neptune symbolizes his goals and dreams. The conjunction in the natal chart indicates that his dreams and goals are closely tied to his work, to the action he takes. This tie is even closer than average because of the conjunction. Because Pluto by transit has passed over both these planets, some career changes are in order, but he may not know what they are yet. He won't know until Pluto forces him out of his reverie when it goes over his Ascendant.

The Ascendant is at 1° Scorpio. Pluto has just entered a ten degree orb to it. He is just beginning to be touched by the Plutonic transformational energy. During the period when Pluto works toward the Ascendant, he will begin to change. His life style and circumstances are symbolized by the Ascendant, so is any new beginning, and how he puts his best foot forward in his career. Pluto will arrive at 1° Scorpio on December 19, 1983. It will retrograde back and forth for several more years. This indicates that phenomenal changes will take place as far as his lifestyle is concerned.

He may feel uprooted; he may feel that he has no control over what he is doing; he may feel that his career is going down the drain and he is helpless to do anything about it. He may feel that he is not standing on dry land, that he is constantly treading water trying to hold his place. This transit is similar to that of Pluto affecting the natal Sun. It is disruptive and it eliminates all the unnecessary elements in the life style. People make big changes under this transit. If he understands the purpose of the transit he can work with it ahead of time.

He must change on this one. We cannot make a client change, though. All we can do is apprise him that change is necessary and leave him to make the decision. The transit causes uneasiness because the energy is not obvious. It is subtle and, as I mentioned under the section describing Pluto transits to the angles, it requires that we give up and let go of the past. That is sometimes very hard to do. But it has to be done, and he will do it voluntarily or he will lose what he no longer needs.

• *Neptune*

Neptune is the next slow moving planet on the list, and on January 1, 1980 it sits at 20° Sagittarius. By transit it sits in his second house. He has three Mutable planets in the signs of Virgo, Gemini and Pisces. None of them are being affected by Neptune at the present because the highest degree in Mutable signs is 14°. So the effect of the transiting Neptune is simply to activate second house matters.

The second house symbolizes things like income, natural talent, our inherent ideas, our values. Neptune brings inspiration and delusion to whatever it touches. He may have highly idealized goals. He may dream and fantasize about making money. He may be inspired to explore his natural talents, to develop his creativity. He can also be completely deluding himself about his income potential. As you question him about income, you'll see how the transit is affecting him. And then you can counsel him based on what he needs to hear.

His income may be slipping through his fingers, or he may not really be concerned with income. You could discuss his financial needs and how he is supporting them. It is important that he consider developing his creative talent now, because the natural energy is there for it and it will not be there after January of 1985. Anything he does to develop this talent will be useful later.

• *Uranus*

This transit is not activating his chart either. It sits at 24° Scorpio on January 1, 1980. He has one Fixed planet at 16° Leo (Pluto). The Uranus transit has passed that point and is sitting in the first house. This brings opportunity for different kinds of work, a multitude of career opportunities, many chances for new beginnings. Although the work opportunities are available, they don't all pan out. If you go back in the ephemeris, you'll find that Uranus hit his Ascendant in December of 1974. This period, from 1974 until the end of 1980 should be an exciting period for career.

Uranus transits are difficult, for when it transits the first house, it brings opportunities but they don't all hold water. It's wise to accept all offers and sit back to determine which one will work. If you say yes to one offer, rejecting all the rest, you may find that you wind up with nothing. So this would be a period where I would recommend accepting all the offers, and walking on eggs until the time presents itself to make a decision.

His second house is 29° Scorpio. Uranus will arrive there in January of 1981. This will activate the second house income potential, bringing more chances for income. Again, these chances may be many and none of them may prove valid. This teaches us how to cope with unpredictability. It teaches us not to put all our eggs in one basket. The transit should bring in business.

So far, there are no really heavy crisis periods in the immediate future. Although the Pluto transit is approaching the Ascendant, this client hasn't really begun to feel the pressure yet. I would begin to wonder why he wants a reading, because usually clients are under greater pressure when they make appointments with me. He may be coming because a friend recommended it; or he may be coming because he doesn't have the transiting energy necessary to help him handle some contemporary problem.

• *Saturn*

Saturn is the transit that teaches us how we need to mature now. It tells us what part of the personality, or what part of our chart, needs attention. On January 1, 1980, Saturn is at 26° Virgo. Although he has three planets in Mutable signs, the highest degree is 14, so he has no real heavy Saturn pressure either.

Saturn is transiting through his eleventh house of friends and advisors. This indicates that he has been spending some time re-evaluating what friends are, what friendship means to him, what kinds of advisors he wants. He should have been making changes regarding friends; he should have begun to become more discriminating. This facet of life can be depressing for we don't like to end friendships— especially since he's a Cancerian, and Cancerians have a tendency to hang on to the past. The weeding out process will continue until December 11, 1980.

The maturation process reflected by the Saturn transit will bring some more serious changes into focus during the coming year. On January 1, 1980, Saturn is at 26° Virgo and it's beginning to activate his Cardinal planets. His natal Uranus is at 5° Cancer. Saturn is approaching the Cardinal sign of Libra. It went into a ten degree orb to Uranus on November 20, 1979 when it hit 25° Virgo. Saturn will go on to activate the natal aspects between his Mercury, Mars, Moon, Sun and Neptune. These planets are all tied together in a t-square. The Saturn energy will hit Uranus until February 14, 1980. Then it retrogrades for a while, and returns on August 17, 1980. It will hit his planets in a domino effect until October 21, 1981.

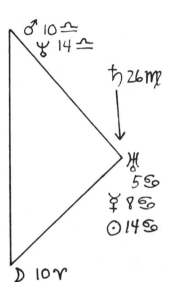

Right now he's not feeling too much pressure but he will shortly. It will build in intensity as Saturn approaches his Moon and Sun. This may be a period he won't enjoy too much, but he certainly will be a stronger person when he comes out of it. If he handles his Saturn energy maturely, if he learns his lessons, this can be an excellent growing period. Because so much of his personality is being activated at one time, under one transit, he may not like it very much at the beginning.

It would be a good idea to go back into the various sections that discuss each transit individually. Let's look at them from a bird's-eye view for the moment. When Saturn squares natal Uranus, it indicates that immature behavior will no longer be accepted. Uranus in Cancer says "I behave like a little boy/big daddy." It would indicate that he exhibits qualities of Cancer that will no longer be accepted, such as that of being too emotional, too possessive, too sensitive, too childish. Saturn comes along and says, "Grow up." We don't have to furrow our brow to figure out where the immaturity comes from. Someone will come along and tell us.

The Saturn transit also activates Uranus square the natal Moon and a natal square to Mars. This may indicate that he takes overly emotional or self destructive action in some way. Because Uranus also conjuncts natal Mercury, he may be overly wordy, he may jump to conclusions, he may say things that he regrets later. During this transit, he'll be called on his immaturity. It needs to be let go.

Saturn moves on to square Mercury, the Moon and Mars. These planets are so close together, it's impossible to separate them. Saturn transiting his Mercury says he must change how he communicates. He'll begin to choose his words more carefully; he'll try to reach people with words and when he doesn't feel he is doing so he may shut up and withdraw. Some loss of concentration may take place. He may sound harsh to others. He may seem cold and withdrawn. The problem is that he will be feeling the futility of communication. It's hard to reach another with words and during this transit we try to do it. The transit is further complicated by natal aspects to Mercury. The square to Mars indicates that he doesn't listen before he jumps to conclusions; the conjunction with Uranus further emphasizes that he jumps to conclusions before checking out the situation; the square to the Moon indicates that he argues rather than communicating his feelings. This transit will teach him something about changing his communication habits. It may be the the people he lives with won't accept his rash choice of words anymore. They will become his Saturn.

When Saturn conjuncts his Mars, he'll feel his activities restricted. He may have difficulty getting work, or the work itself involves restriction. He may not feel his career is all that it should be. He may also feel that his sex drive is changing; he may incorporate a feeling of responsibility along with sex. Sex may become more meaningful to him than it has before.

Saturn opposing the Moon indicates a difficult period with the women in his life. His emotional needs are changing, and he'll be looking for more love and affection. Again, this won't be a need for sex as much as it is a need to be understood and hugged. Cancerians need that anyway. But this transit will intensify the need.

His relationships with women are going to change. He may lose a female friend; he may have a misunderstanding with a female friend that costs him a relationship; he may break up with his girlfriend; he may become estranged from his mother or a female relative. Someone he knows and loves may die and the chances are it will be a woman. During this transit, I recommend that my clients stay in touch with mother, or the favorite aunt or grandmother. If any of these relatives are going to pass over, this is the year to give them the time and affection they need. This is the time to let those you love know that you love them, because it's hard to do when they are no longer here.

This transit teaches us something about Platonic love. He will be learning about love in its less personal form during this transit. And the women in his life will be teaching him.

Along with a feeling of loss goes a feeling of depression because his emotional needs won't be satisfied. As we re-evaluate what those emotional needs are, we are confronted with the fact that we are not happy with the status quo, for we are no longer getting what we need. This is an excellent period for working, for getting ahead in the career area, because not much else is happening. He may be more tired than usual, because when Saturn transits the Moon, we need to take care of ourselves more. We need more sleep; we don't have the endurance that we once had. His natal Moon is in the sixth house, also indicating a need to take better care of himself as far as health is concerned.

Saturn will be conjuncting his natal Neptune and squaring his Sun at the same time. When it passes over Neptune, it brings some depression and feelings of hopelessness. Saturn is a crystallizing energy, and as it hits Neptune it begins to crystallize our dreams and hopes and goals. That is an area of the life that most people don't discuss easily. We don't like to put too much reality around our dreams and goals; we like to leave them shimmering in fantasy. Perhaps we're afraid that reality will show the cigarette burns in the fabric of our gown of illusion. But it is necessary that he re-evaluate his goals now, as Saturn is forcing him to do it.

Pluto is going over the Ascendant, forcing a change in life style, forcing some change to take place as far as career is concerned. Saturn is sitting on Neptune saying look at your goals, look at your dreams. Is that what you want? Is that where you're going? The dream needs to be adjusted; he needs to take a new look at what he is trying to be, what he is striving for.

Saturn is also squaring his Sun, and when this happens, the most obnoxious qualities of the Sun sign are brought to the fore. We are forced to let go of some of these qualities, especially as they don't help us get where we are going. Because he is a Cancerian, he will be looking at the less than lovable qualities of Cancer. These qualities are usually some facet of over-possessiveness, over-emotionalism, too much of the little boy act or too much of the big daddy role. People won't buy it anymore, so friends, family, co-workers, employers will all refuse to play the game. Some Cancers have a tendency to be parasites and he may have to cope with some aspect of this kind of behavior as well.

The Saturn transit spanks us when we are not mature enough. Not that we haven't been doing alright, but when it's time for us to mature, to let go of old behavior patterns, the Saturn transit restricts us, or blocks us every time we reach out the wrong way. We have to keep changing. Saturn tests us, and pushes us to grow by putting restrictions in our path. We test our mettle by having to handle the transit. As we test ourselves,we become stronger; we become the tested warrior or the mythic hero.

During the year that Saturn hits off his Cardinal planets, he will be in pain, as he is learning a great deal in a short period of time. He has six Cardinal planets, and the Saturn pressure will be difficult. It should be kept in mind, however, that he was born with this chart and is familiar with this kind of pressure. This kind of a transit can activate a new life style, a new career, a new direction in an old career. Both his work and his personal life will change. If he is married, or involved in a relationship, he will have to change how he handles that relationship. Not only does he have to talk about his new emotional needs and concepts, but if he doesn't mature, his partner will become his Saturn!

• *Jupiter*

On January 1, 1980, Jupiter is at 10° Virgo. The Jupiter transit stresses relationships and causes change in how we reach out to others. He has three planets in Mutable signs—natal Jupiter at 7° Pisces, Venus at 11° Gemini and Saturn at 14° Virgo. These three planets form a t-square. They are all activated by the Jupiter transit because this transit is still applying to his natal Saturn. Going back in the ephemeris to see when this mess started, we see that Jupiter hit 27° Leo (ten degrees away from an opposition to natal Jupiter at 7° Pisces) on September 16, 1979.

The natal t-square indicates certain difficulties he may have in pulling the three aspects of his personality together so he can begin to feel comfortable with himself. Jupiter in Pisces says, "I relate like a martyr, I reach out in a very spiritual and sensitive way, and my relationships might cause me some suffering." Venus in Gemini says, "I enjoy controversial or different kinds of things, I appreciate my lover intellectually." This means he may appreciate the person he loves

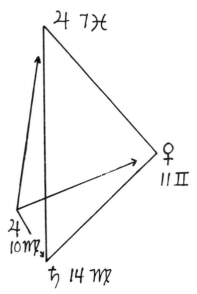

inside his head, but he may have difficulty letting her know how he feels. The Gemini Venus also indicates he may enjoy creating "flack" in a relationship—and his partner may not appreciate his antics. He may pick lovers who are unusual or who have unusual circumstances surrounding the life style. Saturn in Virgo says, "I regard my intellect with caution." Because Saturn sits in the eleventh house natally, he may also limit his friendships, or choose friends who really can't help him. He may choose friends who stand in his way.

The Venus-Jupiter square in the natal chart says that he may over-relate to what he loves; he may not have a perspective. If he enjoys work he may devote too much time to it on a sporadic level; he may over-relate and under-relate as a lover, depending on his mood. This is caused by the effect of Saturn on his natal Jupiter, for Saturn symbolizes closing off and Jupiter symbolizes opening up. These two planets in hard aspect to each other cause us to act like caution lights— blinking on and off. This aspect can confuse the person who has it, as well as those who live around him, because others don't know where he is coming from.

The Saturn-Venus natal square is a serious one, for it indicates that he may be a pessimist about Venus activities. Venus symbolizes the psychological affect of the mother on the developing child. Because he is a male, this would indicate that he picked up, or absorbed an attitude about the feminine principle, about women in general from her. Saturn symbolizes the affect of his father on a psychological level. Because the two planets are square, one may assume that the images of normal man-woman relationships that he absorbed early in life from his parents doesn't give him much optimism about his own. He may have lost everything he was attached to when he was a child, and he may be extremely pessimistic about his adult relationships.

The Jupiter transit is activating all these psychic images. This should be a period of strain and stress for him. The Jupiter transit is conjuncting his natal Saturn, so this could be a time when some of his fears and apprehensions are lightened. This could be a period when he can begin to evaluate some of the father imprint so that he can let go what he doesn't need. He has to be careful, because if he lets go of the father imprint, he doesn't have to choose his mother, and vice versa. These parents don't look as if they offered him much that was constructive about the building of healthy relationships. He will have to learn how to build his own as he matures.

Because transiting Jupiter goes retrograde in the Spring of 1980, this transit will remain activated until August 17, 1980. He can really learn to sort out some of his feelings on this one, although it probably won't feel pleasant. One good thing that comes from a Jupiter transit is that of being actually able to focus on feeling the natal aspect. It can be a pretty intense experience. In the process of self-analysis, this transit can allow us to *feel* the natal aspects so that we can become conscious of the internal pressure that we have been living with since we were born.

After Jupiter goes off the Mutable planets he gets a short rest. On October 4, 1980, Jupiter by transit arrives at 25° Virgo and begins to square his natal Uranus. This transit will activate his Cardinal t-squares. It will hit with a domino affect, going from Uranus, to Mercury, to Mars, Moon, Neptune and Sun. This transit will hit at the same time that the Saturn transit is there, but it won't last as long.

Since the transit of Jupiter has something to do with the relating principle, the hard aspects by transit usually indicate a tendency to overrelate. Jupiter on Uranus indicates a tendency to over-behave; perhaps he'll be jumping to conclusions. Jupiter hitting natal Mercury indicates too much talking; sloppy thinking, perhaps "running off at the mouth" before he's thought about the effect of his words. Jupiter hitting natal Mars indicates too quick a reaction. He may take thoughtless action; he may over-buy. Jupiter hitting the Moon indicates an over-sensitivity. His feelings may be easily hurt. He may lash out at others because he feels so vulnerable. Jupiter hitting the natal Neptune enlivens his dream, or it may cloud it. He may prefer his fantasy to the real world around him. And Jupiter squaring his Sun by transit indicates that he won't be relating well to himself. He may put himself down; he may forget his long range interests because his relating attitude is bad. When this kind of energy is active, we tend to cut off our noses to spite our face. This could affect both relationships and business opportunities.

The cycle breaks on September 17, 1981. Normally a Jupiter transit lasts for about two months. Because of its retrograde and direct motion in the signs of Virgo and Libra, he will be coping with the Jupiterian energy for long periods of time. This is a most frustrating transit. This energy will cause a great deal of inner tension because of the extended period of time that it will be in effect. It would be wise to tell him of the aspect's strength. I have found that the Jupiter transit goes retrograde when it is important for us to learn something about the relating principle.

He has two major t-squares in his chart. His personal planets are all in conflict with each other. This puts a great deal of stress on him. He is a Cancerian which indicates that he is a more emotional type than many other people, and it indicates that his energy is very stressful. In order to become productive he must learn how to handle this inner stress. T-squares indicate the potential for tremendous creativity once we learn how to handle them. We cannot function as victims: we must be in command of our own ship in order for the energy to function in a friendly way. He must accept all the Cardinal energy, and figure out a way for it to operate within him at the same time. He cannot keep suppressing one side of his personality and favoring another. That means he would be in a constant state of repression and suppression, with parts of the personality bursting forth periodically. This causes emotional outbursts, and he won't seem rational. The Jupiter transit can be a period that he uses to begin to really understand himself and his need for personal expression.

The Mutable t-square needs to be expressed as well. So the qualities of Pisces, Virgo and Gemini will have to be incorporated so they can function cooperatively as well. For a better understanding of how this energy will work, see my book *Astrological Insights into Personality* published by Astro Computing Services.

Over the years, I've noticed that the extended Jupiter transit or the extended Mars transit caused real trauma when either of these planets goes retrograde for a long period of time, and it is a difficult one for clients to handle. The Jupiter transit can stretch from two months into a ten month pressure. The Mars transit can stretch from a two week to a five month deal and it causes more problems than a Saturn or a Pluto transit. The energies symbolized by Mars and Jupiter are powerful. The Mars energy symbolizes unchanneled anger, and the Jupiter transit symbolizes unchanneled relating energy. When Jupiter is not used constructively, it turns into a heavy dose of "I don't care." The bad attitude causes people to participate in unconstructive activity that can be quite damaging. When a client has a period of this kind of crisis coming up, I leave the door open. "If you have trouble handling this one, come on back and we'll try to work it out." I'm not scheduling appointments or forcing that person to come back and spend money, but I'm available to listen if he feels he would like to try to sort out his feelings.

After typing up this section, I showed it to my client and we discussed what was said. We didn't really touch on the Jupiter transit, but we talked about the Saturn transit and how Pluto was approaching his Ascendant. He is in the middle of a dilemma at the moment. He has worked in the music business for years, establishing a favorable reputation for himself, but he doesn't like his financial situation. He got an offer from his father to come into the family business. This would give him financial stability and a regular schedule. Working as a musician, he doesn't have financial stability and he doesn't work regularly. His training comes from music—it has been his life until this point. He started playing instruments when he was five; he is now thirty. The dilemma is a painful one.

We talked and talked about the pros and cons of staying a musician and starving to death, constantly traveling, living in hotel rooms, losing out on relationships, etc. We talked about the stability of working in a regular profession and having a profession that he could count on. The battle is between his love for music, his love for playing music, and his interest in becoming stable. This battle applies to his Cancerian Sun, for he wants security—the security that a close relationship and steady money can create. And he wants (Gemini) to be a star—to have audiences know who he is. His father's business won't do that for him.

He has to make up his mind by the end of 1980 because his father can't wait any longer. His transits don't indicate that he will really know what he wants to do until 1983. So he's on his own about this decision. Had the transits been different, he might have been able to look forward to some feelings of definition earlier. But Pluto is approaching his Ascendant, Saturn hasn't gone over his Neptune yet, and it hasn't contacted his Sun yet. So he's in a dilemma.

The decision is made even more difficult because of the Jupiter transit he's under. Although Jupiter going over his Saturn should lighten up some of his Saturnian fears and cautions, he's also coping with developing a new image of what he considers authority to be. And working with his father, an authority figure, will not be easy, because he's a bit of a rebel. The battle is between giving up the rebelliousness and going into the world of tradition and authority; or moving from music which is rebellious into the traditional business world. He could do either, because his chart indicates that he could work well where ever he places his loyalties, but he has to decide that for himself.

We also discussed his Saturn transit, and his pessimism regarding relationships. This comes from the Saturn-Venus natal square, but it is being set off by transit. He was feeling that if he didn't make the "right" decision that his relationship with his wife would end. He didn't say that she was pushing him—for he felt that she was standing back allowing him to make the decision for himself. But he felt that he might lose her if he didn't make the decision to "go traditional." When we discussed the possibility of that part of his life working out—that he didn't have to give her up, that if he vascillated back and forth, she might still be available to him—he began to smile. He said, "You know, I have a fantasy about my relationship. It's about it ending. And I'll pack my suitcase and leave. With nothing. Just a little suitcase. And I'll say, 'You can keep my instruments, you can sell them or something.' And then I go off into the streets—alone."

As we discussed the natal Saturn-Venus square, we also talked about the fact that he didn't have to lose what he loved. He didn't have to give it up. Jupiter transiting his Saturn-Venus square at the moment indicates a time when he can think about his pessimism, and maybe give the pessimism up. He doesn't have to lose out on relationships. He doesn't have to have the kind of relationships that his parents had. He can have any kind of relationship that he wishes to establish—but he'll have to give something to it. He'll have to learn how to talk to the person he loves. He has a natal Mercury-Moon square, so he didn't learn how to do this when he was a child—he never saw his mother really communicating her feelings to his father. But these things can be learned if he wants to.

Again, you can see that the client is not interested in discussing all his transits. His immediate situation was uppermost on his mind. I didn't know that he was under this kind of pressure. But when he started telling me what it was, I could relate to the dilemma, because I knew where the transits were. He is feeling the changes coming. His apprehension is happening because he's feeling them and he can't put his finger on the feeling yet.